I've decided to become Catholic.

Chocolate seems to be a popular choice for Lenten denial. This is something I find hard to understand. I can't go more than twelve hours without chocolate. And that's the twelve hours when I'm sleeping.

Tommy studiously ignores his mom and turns his attention to me. His eyes are even bluer than Mac's.

"So what have you given up, Justine?" he asks.

"She's Jewish, you idiot," Mac interjects. "She doesn't have to give up anything."

"Actually, I've given up being Jewish for Lent," I say, in what I hope is a breezy, casual manner.

I realize I haven't achieved it when four sets of blue eyes stare at me from around the table. There is an awkward moment of shocked silence.

"Now why would you want to do that, Justine?" Mrs. McAllister asks gently, leaving the dishwasher to come sit at the table. "Debbie, one of my best friends from college, is Jewish. I used to wish I were, too."

Wild. I never imagined anyone would *want* to be Jewish....

OTHER BOOKS YOU MAY ENJOY

Bird	Angela Johnson
The Cat Ate My Gymsuit	Paula Danziger
Dizzy	Cathy Cassidy
Eleven	Lauren Myracle
Getting Near to Baby	Audrey Couloumbis
Gossip Times Three	Amy Goldman Koss
LBD: It's a Girl Thing	Grace Dent
A Long Way from Chicago	Richard Peck
Notes from a Liar and Her Dog	Gennifer Choldenko
Squashed	Joan Bauer
Thwonk	Joan Bauer
A Year Down Yonder	Richard Peck

Confessions of a Closet Catholic

Confessions of a

Closet Catholic

SARAH
DARER
LITTMAN

PUFFIN BOOKS

PUFFIN BOOKS
Published by the Penguin Group
Penguin Young Readers Group,
345 Hudson Street, New York, New York 10014, U.S.A.
Penguin Group (Canada), 90 Eglinton Avenue East, Suite 700, Toronto,
Ontario, Canada M4P 2Y3 (a division of Pearson Penguin Canada Inc.)
Penguin Books Ltd, 80 Strand, London WC2R 0RL, England
Penguin Ireland, 25 St Stephen's Green, Dublin 2, Ireland
(a division of Penguin Books Ltd)
Penguin Group (Australia), 250 Camberwell Road, Camberwell, Victoria 3124, Australia
(a division of Pearson Australia Group Pty Ltd)
Penguin Books India Pvt Ltd, 11 Community Centre, Panchsheel Park,
New Delhi - 110 017, India
Penguin Group (NZ), Cnr Airborne and Rosedale Roads, Albany,
Auckland 1310, New Zealand (a division of Pearson New Zealand Ltd)
Penguin Books (South Africa) (Pty) Ltd, 24 Sturdee Avenue, Rosebank,
Johannesburg 2196, South Africa

Registered Offices: Penguin Books Ltd, 80 Strand, London WC2R 0RL, England

First published in the United States of America by Dutton Children's Books,
a division of Penguin Young Readers Group, 2005
Published by Puffin Books, a division of Penguin Young Readers Group, 2006

1 3 5 7 9 10 8 6 4 2

This book is a work of fiction. Names, characters, places, and incidents are either the product of the author's imagination or are used fictitiously, and any resemblance to actual persons, living or dead, business establishments, events, or locales is entirely coincidental.

CIP Data is available.

Puffin Books ISBN 0-14-240597-3

Designed by Irene Vandervoort

Printed in the United States of America

Dedicated to Joshua and Amie,
the inspiration for everything I do.

And to the late
Lieutenant Commander Peter Palm,
who always had something to say about religion.

Finally, this book is dedicated to the late
Paula Danziger—"yenta," mentor, and friend.
I hope someday I can give even a fraction of the
warmth, generosity, and humor that my
"writing mom" showed to young children and
new writers alike. Paula, you are deeply missed.

Acknowledgments

My sincerest and grateful thanks to:
Jim Wolfe, Features Editor at the *Greenwich Time,* for giving me the thrill of seeing my name in print for the first time and encouraging me to keep writing. Also, Mike Sweeney, Editorial Page Editor, for giving me the opportunity to have a "voice" and get paid for it.

My critique group, led by the inestimable Diana Klemin. I salute my comrades-at-arms Bill Buschel, Susan Warner, Dr. Alan Shulman, Lisa Daur, and Gay Morris. Thanks for reminding me when to shut up and let Jussy do the talking. I couldn't have done this without you.

My "Test Readers": Madeleine Abbott, Alex Koones, Lexy Milstein, and teacher extraordinaire, Miss Carrelliene Westbrook.

Barbarann Feeney, Paula Cummings, Marianne Wallace, Tobias Ostapchuk, and the Reverend Michael Moynihan of St. Michael the Archangel R.C. Church, for patiently answering my questions about Catholicism.

Rabbi Yossi and Maryashie Deren of Chabad of Greenwich, for their patient teaching, spiritual guidance, and unstinting support.

Greenwich Library, for providing a conducive atmosphere and, best of all, a clean desk.

And last but certainly not least:

Jodi Reamer, my very own "Super Ultra Secret Agent Network."

My editor, Julie Strauss-Gabel, who by asking the right questions made this book infinitely better than it started out.

Most of all, Cedric and my family (which includes our very own "Mary Poppins," Lindsay Cullingford), for believing in me and cheering me on every step of the way.

Confessions of a Closet Catholic

Chapter One

It's Friday night, and Mom is yelling at me because I won't eat the chicken she cooked for dinner. In our house, Friday night means Sabbath, and Sabbath means chicken. Chopped chicken liver on challah, followed by chicken soup with matzo balls, then roast chicken as the main course. You'd think they'd have come up with some chicken thing for dessert, but it's usually fruit salad, not chicken salad.

Mom doesn't understand that I can't eat chicken on Friday for the next few weeks because I've given up chicken for Lent.

You see, I've decided to become Catholic like my new best friend, Mary Catherine McAllister, otherwise known as Mac. She's given up chocolate for Lent. I don't think God wants me to make that kind of sacrifice. So I've given up being Jewish. And chicken. I just haven't told my parents yet.

It's partly because the last time I tried to talk to my family about religion, it ended in disaster. We were having dinner with Mom's parents, Grandpa Leo and Grandma Lila, at my grandparents' country club, Burning Beeches. It's a Jewish club, but the dinner buffet's always piled high with shrimp and lobster, and other stuff the Torah says Jewish people aren't supposed to eat because it's not kosher.

My "old" best friend from New Rochelle, Shira Weinstein, keeps kosher. At her house they have separate sets of dishes because you're not supposed to mix milk and meat together.

I always thought it would be cool to keep kosher like Shira and Bubbe, my grandma on my dad's side. But when I made the mistake of telling my family that I was thinking about doing it, Grandpa Leon nearly choked on his shrimp.

"What kind of *mishegas* are you talking now, Justine?" he sputtered, dripping cocktail sauce onto his chin.

Right away, I knew I'd made a mistake. I could tell Grandpa was upset because he used Yiddish. He and Grandma Lila only speak it when they don't want us to understand what they're saying, or if they're upset and it slips out by accident.

Miss Perfect (a.k.a. my sister, Helena), and my little brother, Jake, were snickering. If there's one thing you can count on, it's that my brother and sister LOVE to see me humiliated.

Another thing you can count on is that I start to blush the minute I get embarrassed. I was embarrassed that my grandfather thought I was crazy and hurt that he added the *now,* like my bringing up crazy stuff is a regular occurrence.

"Why would you want to take up with those old-fashioned

dietary laws?" Grandma Lila said. "They might have made sense thousands of years ago in the desert, when they didn't have refrigerators, but they don't apply today."

I looked to my father, hoping for some support, because even though we don't keep kosher in our house (much to Bubbe's dismay), he at least was brought up that way. But Dad just sat there eating. It would take an argument of nuclear proportions to come between Dad and his food. He says that it's because Bubbe and my late Grandpa Sam, whom we called Zayde, were in a concentration camp during World War II. They were always hungry. Afterward, they always worried about having enough to eat. One of Dad's favorite stories is about how when he was a kid, his parents made him stay at the table until he'd finished everything on his plate, even if it was runny scrambled eggs, which he hates. Mom says finishing everything on his own plate is one thing, but Dad usually finishes everything on everyone else's plate, too.

"Bubbe keeps kosher," I said, without thinking.

Grandma Lila bristled. *Earth to Justine's mouth,* I thought. *Another fine mess you've gotten us into.*

Telling a grandma who *doesn't* do something that you want to do it because the other one *does* is not smart family politics. In fact, it's a recipe for disaster. I seem to be a master chef for *that* kind of recipe.

"Well." Grandma Lila sniffed. "That may be. But I like to think that Judaism in the twenty-first century has evolved beyond that kind of superstitious nonsense."

Grandpa Leo nodded his head in agreement as he bit into a lobster tail. Helena and Jake sat across the table from me, smirking.

"So how about those Yankees?" Dad asked. And that was the end of that.

Afterward, I decided if my family was going to make fun of me for trying to be Jewish, I might as well try something else. I got a book from the school library about world religions and read about some of the alternatives. I read about Islam first. I was surprised at how many similarities there are between Islam and Judaism, although maybe it's understandable since we share a great-great-great-great-great-great—well, thousands of years' worth of greats—grandfather in Abraham.

I liked the idea of covering my hair with a head scarf because then it wouldn't matter that it's so frizzy and out of control. Imagine not having to worry about a bad hair day ever again.

But then I read about Ramadan. You have to fast during the daylight hours for a *whole month*. It's bad enough having to fast for twenty-four hours once a year on Yom Kippur. I can't imagine having to go a whole month being hungry, even if you do get to eat at night.

So I moved on. There are a lot of cool things about Hinduism and Buddhism. They both seem pretty flexible about how you express your faith. Imagine if it were like that in my family. I wouldn't be stuck in the cross fire between Bubbe wanting me to be Jewish the Orthodox (or what my other grandparents would call the "old-fashioned") way, and Grandma Lila and Grandpa Leo wanting me to be Jewish but not "too Jewish."

But then I read the part about "samsara"; how you keep getting reborn over and over until you get it right. If I thought I could be reborn looking like Mom or my sister, Helena, instead of the way I do now, then it wouldn't be so bad. But the thought of having to come back again and again as me, Justine Silver, short, frizzy-haired, and zit-faced (or something worse), is pretty depressing. Plus there are a lot of gods to keep track of, and remembering things isn't my strong suit. I can just see myself calling one of them by the wrong name when I pray and being sentenced to coming back as a cockroach. With my luck, I'd end my next life in a Roach Motel. Nope, I can't be Hindu.

When I tried to be Buddhist and meditate, instead of achieving a relaxed and spiritual state of mind, all I could think of was the enormous zit starting to erupt on my chin, my itchy nose, the fact my butt was starting to hurt from sitting cross-legged on the floor, and how much I wanted some of the Swiss chocolate Dad brought back from a business trip.

By the time I started trying to calculate the chocolate/zit ratio (how many squares of chocolate you have to eat to produce one zit), I realized that I wasn't going to cut it as a Buddhist.

I never realized that Christianity was made up of so many different denominations until I looked stuff up about it on the Internet. There's something like thirty-four thousand different Christian groups worldwide. You've got the Protestants, Catholics, Eastern Orthodox, Baptists, Adventists, Amish, Christian Scientists, Methodists, and Lutherans. And that's only naming a few. I thought that everyone who believed in Jesus worshiped pretty much the same way, but there are a lot of differences. I couldn't figure out which was the best thing to be.

So in the end I decided to be a Catholic like Mac, at least for Lent, and I'm not going to eat my chicken, because you're not supposed to eat meat on Fridays during the Lenten period. Since the entire Sabbath meal revolves around chicken (chicken counts as meat, doesn't it?), Mom's mad.

Helena looks up from the lettuce leaf that she toys with on her plate, and gives my mother a sympathetic glance.

"Maybe Jussy's decided to be vegetarian like me." She

sniffs in a superior tone. "But it's probably just another one of her phases, like wanting to keep kosher."

She looks at me and smirks. "Whatever will she think up next?"

My little brother, Jake, sniggers. Mom rolls her eyes. One thing that gets me mad about my family is that they never take me seriously. That's just one thing. I made a list once of all the things that get me down about my family. It's pretty long, but here's the top five: 1) My mother loves my sister more than me. 2) My dad loves my brother more than me. 3) My mother loves her miniature poodle, Bijoux, more than me. 4) Mom is tall, thin, blond, and beautiful. (So is Helena. I got the short, brown, and dumpy genes. *WHY?!*) 5) Nobody in my family takes me seriously.

"I'm not becoming vegetarian," I protest angrily. "I'm . . ."

The confession is poised on the tip of my tongue. But, I chicken out. Chickening out is the only kind of chicken I'm allowed during Lent.

"I'm just not hungry," I mutter.

My mother looks skeptical. She gives me the Raised Eyebrow.

"Sure you're not," Jake taunts me. "You just scarfed five big matzo balls, even if you didn't eat the soup."

"Shut up, *Dog Breath!*" I hiss, kicking him under the table for emphasis.

Jake doesn't take it like a man.

"Justine kicked me!" he whines.

"Justine Frieda Silver!" Mom says in That Voice.

I know I'm in trouble when Mom uses That Voice, and it's even more serious when she uses my middle name, because she knows how much I hate it. My middle name's another of the injustices heaped upon me by my parents, who gave Helena a pretty middle name, Grace.

I put my head down and start to eat my green beans. Maybe if I eat my vegetables, Mom will forget about the chicken.

The phone rings.

"I'll get it," I say, leaping up before Helena moves, even though I know it's probably for her.

Sure enough, it is. It's a boy. He sounds embarrassed.

"Um . . . is, uh . . . can I talk to . . . uh, Helena?" he mumbles.

I'm sick of the way guys get all stupid around my sister, and I'm mad that the phone is always for her and never for me.

"Sorry, she's not here," I say, and hang up the phone without asking who it is.

Back in the dining room, Helena asks who was on the phone.

"Some boy," I tell her. "I told him you weren't here."

Helena shrieks with rage.

"*MOM! DAD!* Can you *believe* what she did?"

She's noisy enough that Dad actually looks up from his food to give me an angry look. He tells me to go to my room with no dessert. Right. Like I'm going to cry about missing fruit salad.

I detour through the kitchen on my way upstairs and sneak a few matzos and a bottle of grape juice. Not because I'm hungry. I need them to practice.

Once in my room, I lock the door and change into a long black skirt and a plain black T-shirt. It's the closest thing I have to a nun's habit. I take the starched white napkin I stole from the linen closet out of its hiding place in my sweater drawer and pin it to the top of my head with bobby pins, folding the corners down behind my ears. I pretend I look like a nun, instead of an eleven-going-on-twelve-year-old Jewish girl with a dinner napkin on her head.

There's a flashlight in my bedside table and I take it into the closet, which thankfully is a decent size in this house, not shoebox-size like my closet in our old house in New Rochelle. Switching on the flashlight, I close the door and sit down. Hidden in a sock inside a pair of hideous patent-leather shoes that I hate but Mom insisted on buying me is a set of rosary beads. I bought them at Revelations, the store downtown that sells all kinds of religious stuff. There's also a small silver cross necklace that Mac left at my house when she slept over. She asked me if I'd found it, and I lied and said no.

I put on the necklace, and feel a familiar pang of guilt. I haven't worked out if it's because I lied to Mac or because whenever I put it on, I picture the look on Bubbe's face if she ever saw me wearing it.

But guilt is good. It gets me in the mood to confess. Confession is the reason I'm sitting on the floor of my closet. Despite the fact that it's a mess of shoes, clothes, and dirty laundry, it serves as my confessional.

"Forgive me, Father, for I have sinned. It's been three days, fifteen hours, thirty-seven minutes, and about fifteen seconds since my last confession," I whisper to the enormous teddy bear that Zayde bought me when he took me to FAO Schwarz in New York for my fifth birthday.

Father Ted looks at me without saying anything, waiting for me to fess up.

"I lied to some boy about my sister not being home. I kicked my brother, Jake, even if he did ask for it. My parents are mad at me for all of the above, and because I won't eat chicken," I tell him.

Father Ted hasn't learned his lines, so I have to play both parts.

"Anything else?" I ask in my deep Father Ted voice.

Mac tells me that she always makes up a few sins to tell her priest so she doesn't sound like a goody-goody. If I had a Mom like Mrs. McAllister, and nice brothers and sisters like

Mac's, I'd probably have to make up sins, too. As it is, I always have a long list of bad things I've done, even if most of them *were* because I was provoked.

So I tell Father Ted how I borrowed Helena's favorite T-shirt without asking when a group of us went to the movies and how some jerk smoking in the line behind me burned a hole in the shoulder. I tell him how I've lied to both my sister and my mother, telling them that I haven't seen the T-shirt, when actually I know I buried it at the bottom of the trash can in the garage the night before the garbage men came.

Father Ted sighs.

"My child, my child," he says sadly. In his deep priestly voice he instructs me to do penance.

"Ten Hail Marys. And meditate on your actions," he tells me.

Clutching the rosary beads, I dig into the sock again and take out a small piece of paper on which I've copied the Hail Mary. Shining the flashlight on it, I read:

"Hail, Mary, full of grace, the Lord is with thee; blessed art thou among women and blessed is the fruit of thy womb . . ."

I stumble, as always, over the word *Jesus.* I don't know if it's being the granddaughter of Holocaust survivors, or if it's my Jewish genes rebelling against my closet conversion; I feel guilty saying the J-word when I pray. But I figure Mary is going to know who I'm talking about since he's the fruit of her womb, so I continue.

"Holy Mary . . ."

I stumble again. I have problems with the "Mother of God" part, too. I mean if God is God, and if He created the universe and everything in it, then how can Mary be His mother? I need Catholic lessons to understand it. I tried asking Mac once, but she confused me even more by bringing the Holy Ghost into the equation.

Deciding to skip the M-O-G, I continue.

"Pray for us now and at the hour of our death. Amen."

After I've repeated this, minus the J-word and the M-O-G phrase, another nine times, Father Ted tells me it's time for Communion.

I take one of the matzos I brought up from the kitchen, and carefully pour grape juice into a Dixie Cup. Father Ted and I haven't got the Communion part down yet. I've never seen it done in real life, only on TV. So we improvise. I eat a bit of matzo and take a slug of the grape juice. Then Father Ted mumbles "Body and Blood of Christ" a few times because that's all he knows about Communion.

I'm busy munching on my Communion matzo-wafer when I hear banging on the bedroom door, which thankfully I remembered to lock.

"Hey, Jussy!" comes Jake's high-pitched voice. "I've got something for you."

When I don't answer, hoping he'll go away, he bangs a few more times.

"Why'd you lock your door? What're you doing in there?"

I open the closet door a few inches and shout, "Go away, Jake!"

He rattles on the door handle, as if by some magic or the brute strength of his eight-year-old hands, the door will suddenly go open sesame.

"C'mon. Open up! I've got a present for you," he pleads.

It's always hard to know about Jake and his presents. Sometimes he can be surprisingly sweet. Other times he'll pretend he's got a present for me and it'll be a dead dragonfly or a caterpillar or something else creepy and boylike.

I figure maybe he's trying to make up for getting me into trouble at dinner, so I tuck Mac's cross under the collar of my T-shirt and crawl out of the closet, carefully closing the door to conceal Father Ted and the remnants of my matzo-and-grape-juice Communion.

When I unlock the door to my room, Jake holds out two oatmeal-raisin cookies from Ambrosia, the organic store in town. They're my favorite, and he knows it. Now I feel *genuinely* repentant about kicking him in the shin at dinner.

"I thought you might be upset about missing dessert," he says awkwardly.

I'm in the middle of thanking him and telling him that he's a pretty good brother after all, when I notice he's staring at the top of my head. Reaching up, I realize I forgot to take off the napkin. Uh-oh. I rip it off my head and stuff it into the pocket of my skirt.

"Uh, Jussy . . ." Jake says hesitantly, like he's afraid to upset our newly found peace. "Why were you wearing one of Mom's fancy napkins on your head?"

Fortunately, I'm pretty good at thinking on my feet.

"We're studying English history," I lie. "We're doing a skit about Queen Elizabeth the First, and I'm practicing for my role as Mary Queen of Scots."

He's still looking at me kind of funny, so I throw in the kind of gross, historical tidbit that I know will distract him.

"She's the one who tried to take over Queen Elizabeth's throne and ended up getting her head chopped off."

I've just finished confessing, and within minutes of leaving my closet confessional I'm already lying. What's even scarier is how good I am at it. I wonder if Mac finds it this hard to remain sin-free.

"You're going to get your head chopped off? Cool!" Jake says, buying my deception and moving on to what really matters to him. "Hey, do you want to play S.U.S.A.N. with me?"

Super Ultra Secret Agent Network, or S.U.S.A.N., is Jake's favorite video game. I hate to admit that I like anything my little brother likes, but it's a blast to play. Each player is a spy from a different country. You have to capture the Ultra Top Secret Formula that gives your country the Power to Rule the World.

I give Jake a noogie. "Okay, but only if I get to be Hungary."

I always like to be Hungary because that's where Bubbe lived with her parents, nine brothers and sisters, and scores of cousins before the war. Bubbe was the only one of them who survived. Sometimes when we play S.U.S.A.N. I imagine finding the Top Secret Formula in time to Rule the World and defeat Hitler. Then the tattoo on Bubbe's arm, the one they put on her in the concentration camp, disappears, and suddenly we have lots of uncles, aunts, and cousins.

"How can you be hungry?" Jakey says in his lame attempt at a joke. "I just brought you two cookies."

"Shut up," I say affectionately, and we go into his room to play.

Chapter Two

I was really upset last summer when Mom and Dad said we were moving to Greenwich, Connecticut, from New Rochelle, New York, where we'd lived my whole life. I loved our house, even if it was much smaller than the one we live in now. We lived on a street where there were lots of other kids my age. Shira lived three blocks away, and it was safe enough for me to go there on my bike, so I didn't have to plead for rides from my parents like I do now whenever I want to go anywhere.

Shira has a little brother, Sammy, who is a year younger than Jake and almost as much of a pain, and her mom and my mom are good friends, even though her family is a lot more observant of all the Jewish traditions than mine. Rain or shine, Shira's family walks to synagogue every Saturday morning, because observant Jews don't drive a car or use anything mechanical or electrical on the Sabbath, which runs from sundown on Friday evening until an hour after sundown on Saturday night.

My parents hardly ever go to services, much less walk there. In the winter, services conflict with Mom's exercise class and Helena's art class, and in the spring and fall with Jake's soccer practice. It's hard having your Sabbath on a day when most people are shopping and getting on with life.

Back in New Rochelle, when Bubbe came to stay with us for the weekend and the weather wasn't too bad for her arthritis, I'd walk with her over to the Weinsteins' house on Saturday morning, then we'd all go to synagogue together. She'd try to get the rest of my family to come, but they always had some excuse. That seemed to make Bubbe sad. She'd sigh and mutter something under her breath in Yiddish as she put her wrinkled hand on my arm.

"Come, *bubbele,*" she'd say in her heavily accented voice, wincing slightly as she walked down the steps. She has a bad back from being kicked by a guard when she was in the camp, and now that she's older, the arthritis makes it even worse. "You and I will go."

Even before we moved here, Bubbe hadn't come to synagogue with me for a while. She fell in her apartment and broke her hip. Now, even though she's better, she has to walk with a cane, and from the look on her face when she does, I think it's pretty painful. Dad offered to drive her, but she always refused.

"I've never driven to *shul* in my life. At seventy-five, I'm not going to start," she repeated whenever Dad tried to persuade her to accept a ride. Bubbe has always observed Sabbath, like the Weinsteins, except when she was in the camps and forced to work. Dad says that quitting doing things for Shabbat was fine in the olden days, but as modern people living in America, we shouldn't have to do things like that. It's one of the few things he and Grandma Lila agree on.

I miss going to synagogue with Bubbe. She always kept candies in her pocket, and she'd share them with Shira and me, giving a few to Sammy before he went off to the men's section with Mr. Weinstein.

My parents are what people call "twice a year" Jews. They only see the inside of the synagogue twice a year on the two biggest holidays, Rosh Hashanah, when we celebrate the Jewish New Year, and Yom Kippur, the Day of Atonement, when we're supposed to repent for all of our sins and ask for God's forgiveness so He'll inscribe us in the Book of Life for the coming year.

I think doing confession every week, like Mac does, is a lot better than saving it all up for one day. It's impossible to remember a whole year's worth of sins, especially when you have a family as annoying as mine and are constantly being provoked to do bad things.

Weekly confession was just one of the reasons I decided to become Catholic. Here are some of the others:

1) I get to celebrate Christmas. I still feel weird about the Jesus part of things, but I've always wanted to have a Christmas

tree and decorate the bushes with colored lights. Around here, our house sticks out like a sore thumb because it's dark. I bet people drive by and think, *That's where the Jewish family lives.* It'd be nice to feel like part of the crowd instead of an outsider for a change. It's bad enough feeling on the edge of things because I'm short, fat, and zit prone. But Christmas Day can feel pretty lonely for anyone who's Jewish, even tall, blond, thin Jews like Helena. We go to the movies and eat Chinese food along with the other Jewish families in town, but it's hard when you know that 90 percent of the population is opening presents and drinking eggnog and you're not. For our only chocolate-related festival, Hanukkah, we only get bags of *gelt*, or chocolate coins. Christians get Easter bunnies and eggs filled with even more chocolates. Plus they get those yummy Marshmallow Peeps things. 2) I like the music. Church music is a lot more cheerful than synagogue music. I guess when you've been persecuted for thousands of years, it's hard to write upbeat tunes. 3) Catholic families are more normal than Jewish ones.

Okay, so the last one is probably a sweeping generalization, and as Shira's Dad is fond of saying, "Generalizations are generally wrong." So, let's put it this way: Mac's family is way more normal than my family.

Mac became my other best friend (besides Shira, that is) the first day at my new school, Parkfield. She saw me standing alone in the playground during recess and came over to talk to me.

"Hey, Jessica," she said with a friendly smile. "I'm Mary Catherine, but please call me Mac. You're new here, right?"

I didn't dare tell her my name was really Justine, because I was so glad someone was actually speaking to me.

"Uh, yeah. I'm new. We just moved here from New Rochelle."

"How do you like it so far?" she asked, grabbing hold of the monkey bars and hanging.

I grabbed the monkey bars, too. Monkey See, Monkey Do, especially when it's your first day in a new school and you've felt like a social leper all morning.

"It's okay, I guess," I mumbled.

She was still smiling at me in a friendly sort of way, so I took a chance with the truth.

"Actually, I feel kind of . . . weird," I admitted. "And lonely, I really miss my friends. I don't know anyone here."

"Well, you know me now," she said, as if that settled the matter. "Hey, do you want to come over to my house on Saturday? By the time you've met all my brothers and sisters, you'll feel like you know half the people in Greenwich."

"Why?" I asked curiously. "How many do you have?"

"Well, let's see," she said, dropping from the monkey bars so she could use her fingers to count. "There's Patrick and

Joseph, they're both away at college, then there's Sean, the twins—Teresa and Thomas—and last but not least, me."

"Wow." I didn't know what to say. I'd never met anyone with that many brothers and sisters.

"How 'bout you?" she asked.

"I just have an older sister and a younger brother. I'm stuck in the middle. Say, Mary—"

"Mac. Please call me Mac. The only time I'm ever called Mary Catherine is when I go to confession or if my mother is really, really mad at me."

"What's it like to go to confession?" I asked curiously.

"I don't know. I just go to church and tell the priest what I've done wrong that week. Like hiding Tommy's favorite T-shirt on the night I knew he had a date and wanted to wear it or talking back to my parents. Don't you ever go?"

I could feel myself blushing. "Uh, no. I don't exactly go to church."

She stared at me with what appeared to be envious fascination. "What, your parents never make you go? You are SO lucky. My parents make me go every week without fail. Plus I have to go to CCD during the week."

My face felt hot. I knew I was blushing so much I looked like I'd been on a beach in Tahiti for a week with no sunscreen. And I wasn't sure what CCD was, but there was no way I was going to ask.

"My parents don't go either," I mumbled. "It's because we're . . . um . . . Jewish."

"Oh!" she said. "That explains it."

I got a weird feeling in my stomach.

"Explains what?" I asked, wondering why I felt so defensive all of a sudden.

She stared at me like I had two heads. "*Duh*, Jessica! Why you don't go to church, of course!"

We looked at each other for a few seconds without saying anything, then, at almost exactly the same moment, we burst out laughing.

When I stopped laughing enough to speak, I made a confession of my own.

"Mac?"

"Yes?"

"My name isn't Jessica. It's Justine."

That started Mac giggling again. "Well, thanks for telling me, *Jussica!*"

We've been friends ever since. I've never really understood why Mac picked me for a friend. To look at her, Mac's the kind of girl who'd normally terrify me. She's so perfect-looking, with straight blond hair and blue eyes. I'd have expected her to hang out with all the other pretty, popular girls, instead of wasting her time with a misfit dork like me.

But for some mysterious reason, Mac really likes me.

What's even more amazing is that she's always telling me how *interesting* and *funny* I am. In my whole life no one, except perhaps Bubbe and Shira, has ever found me interesting. I haven't worked out if Mac's suffering from some form of temporary insanity or if she sees something in me that I haven't yet seen in myself. Still, who am I to look a gift friend in the mouth?

So Mac called last night and invited me for a sleepover Saturday night.

"But your mom needs to pick you up by ten-thirty on Sunday morning, because we go to eleven o'clock mass," she said.

"Oh, that's okay," I replied hurriedly, thrilled to have 1) an opportunity to miss Hebrew school, and 2) to get to see a real live mass. "Maybe I could just come to mass with you. Then my parents can pick me up later."

"Are you sure?" Mac said doubtfully. "You won't be bored?"

"It'll be interesting," I told her. And I meant it, too.

When I got off the phone I raced into my room, locked the door, and got in the closet with Father Ted.

"Father Ted, guess what?"

Father Ted is the strong, silent type.

"I'm going to see a real live mass with Mac on Sunday."

He doesn't seem that impressed. Maybe he's holding it against me that I haven't confessed in a day or two. Well, I've had a lot of homework and I've got a book report due Friday that I haven't even started. I figure I'd better do some catching up on the confessing front, especially if I'm going to mass on Sunday. I don't want to be caught in church with sins on my conscience—it would be like getting into an accident wearing dirty underwear.

"Forgive me, Father, for I have sinned," I say to Father Ted. "It's been two days, nine hours, and about forty-nine seconds since my last confession."

I pull a folded piece of paper out from my Secret Sock Stash, something I'd been working on since I looked at the Web site on Catholicism.

"I've made you a checklist of the Seven Deadly Sins," I make Father Ted say in his priest voice. "You can just tick off the ones that apply."

I point the flashlight onto Father Ted's checklist, and pick up the pencil I brought into the closet for this very purpose.

"Let's see now. . . . Envy."

I put a big check by that one. Envy's a biggie for me. I envy my sister, Helena, because she's everything I'm not and because my mom loves her more than me. I envy my brother, Jake, because despite the fact that he's an annoying brat, my dad loves him more than me because he's a *boy.* I even envy Bijoux. You've got to be a pretty sad excuse for a person when you're envious of a dog, especially a runty little puffball like Bijoux.

The next sin on Father Ted's list is sloth. I think about the book report due Friday that I haven't done even though I've known about it for two weeks. So I guess I have to check that one, too.

Greed comes next. I definitely have to check that one. I mean I can't pass by a chocolate bar without wanting it. But does that come under greed or lust?

"Can you lust after chocolate?" I ask Father Ted.

"Put it under greed," replies Father Ted. "And you might as well check off gluttony while you're at it."

Yikes. I'm not doing too well on the sin front. So far I'm four for four. There's got to be *some* sin I haven't committed.

I scan the rest of the checklist. Anger, lust, and pride are left.

"I don't have to check lust, do I?" I ask Father Ted. "That's a grown-up sin."

Father Ted ponders.

"You do spend a little too much time thinking about that pop star with the earring," he says. "But I'll let you off with half a check."

Thank God for small mercies. Finally, there's a sin I've only half committed. I know there's no way I'll get away with skipping anger, because Father Ted knows me too well. But if

I have to list all the reasons I'm mad at my family, I'll be stuck in the closet till the End of Time. Since Father Ted has heard all my grievances before, he lets me off with just a check mark.

"I guess I can give pride a miss," I tell Father Ted sadly. "I don't have a whole lot to be proud of."

"Come now, my child," Father Ted says kindly. "God thinks you're special."

"How does He know?" I argue.

"He's omniscient," Father Ted says, "which means He is infinitely wise and all-knowing."

"I *know* what it means," I snap. "I'm talking to myself, for heaven's sake! But why would He waste His time with a nobody like me?"

"You are His child. And He loves all His children," says Father Ted.

"Too bad my parents don't have that attitude," I mutter.

Father Ted gives me a stern look.

"I was going to give you ten Hail Marys, but I think you'd better make that twenty," he says.

Sighing, I take my Hail Mary cheat sheet out of the sock and start reciting.

By the time I get out of the closet, I'm miserable. Out of the seven worst sins, I've committed five and a half. I'd better get used to life in a very hot climate, because it looks like that's where I'm going to spend eternity.

But at least I have the sleepover at Mac's to look forward to. I love going over to the McAllisters'. The place is always full of kids. You'd think Mrs. McAllister would be fed up with having so many of her own kids around, but she never minds them inviting friends over. Plus they have two golden retrievers, Whiskey and Soda, and a big calico cat named Patches. Whiskey and Soda are *real* dogs that fetch sticks, play ball, and bark at the mailman. They're not stupid little marshmallow fluffs like Bijoux.

Mac's mom is the greatest. She's not uptight about everything being perfect like my mom. Her kitchen has pictures that her kids drew in nursery school stuck to the cupboards, and the phone desk is piled high with recipe books and letters from school. Best of all, she keeps the cookie jar full of homemade cookies, which is amazing considering the number of hands that sneak into it. Her specialty is chocolate-butterscotch-chip cookies, but when she found out that I love oatmeal raisin, she made me some specially. They were even better than the ones Mom buys at Ambrosia. Mac's lucky to have a mom who bakes cookies instead of buying them.

My mother likes the McAllisters, but she hates going to their house. The first time she came to pick me up, Mrs. Mc-

Allister invited her in for coffee and Mom started wheezing within five minutes of sitting down at the McAllisters' huge pine kitchen table. Allergies. She gets asthma if she's around dog or cat hairs. That's why we're stuck with a stupid miniature poodle like Bijoux. She's the only kind of dog Mom's not allergic to.

When we got in the car afterward Mom said, "How can she live that way, in all that mess? And the noise! I think I'm getting a migraine."

Sure enough, the minute we got home she took Bijoux up to her room and went to lie down with the curtains closed and a cold washcloth on her forehead. That's my mom. She has what she calls a "nervous disposition." She hates noise and she hates mess. Mac couldn't believe how neat our house was the first time she came over.

"Wow! This house could be in *Better Homes and Gardens,*" she said. "It's so neat you'd think nobody lives here."

"Nobody does," I told her. "Mom makes us live in a tiny shack at the bottom of the garden so we don't mess the house up."

I was only half joking. Mom goes crazy if any of us leave stuff lying around downstairs. She inspects our rooms every day to make sure they aren't too messy. Even the playroom, which is supposed to be a kid room, has to be tidied to perfection before we go to bed each night.

What I didn't tell Mac is that nothing would make my mom happier than for our house to be featured in *Better Homes and Gardens* or *Greenwich* magazine. She would think she'd died and gone to heaven. And so would Armando and Marcel, the two decorators who are helping her "design the Ultimate Showcase of Tasteful Elegance." Dad says the only designs they have are on his checkbook.

So with the help of Armando and Marcel, our house is being transformed into the "Ultimate Showcase of Tasteful Elegance." But given the choice, I'd take the McAllisters' smaller, messier, noisier house any day.

Chapter Three

On Saturday afternoon Dad drives me to the McAllisters', and he accepts Mrs. McAllister's invitation to come in for coffee. He doesn't seem to mind the mess and the noise. Of course, the fact that Mrs. McAllister always gives him cookies without lecturing him about his weight and his cholesterol levels might have something to do with it, too.

I give Dad a kiss good-bye.

"Don't tell your mother," he mumbles through a mouthful of chocolate-butterscotch-chip cookie.

"Don't worry, Dad," I tell him. "Your secret is safe with me."

Mac is out in the McAllisters' backyard, with Sean and the twins. The McAllisters' backyard is sports heaven. There are two soccer goals set up, a basketball hoop by the driveway, a trampoline, and a badminton set. It's not landscaped to perfection like our house. Mrs. McAllister enjoys doing the gardening herself, and as she says, she has enough built-in labor to do whatever work she needs.

Not long after I met Mac, I went over to her house and

we all helped rake leaves. Halfway through, Mrs. McAllister brought out mugs of hot apple cider with sticks of cinnamon in them. It tasted like autumn in a cup. I had a great time.

Mac says that I only think raking is fun because we have a gardening service that comes with these noisy machines that blow the leaves into neat piles so I never have to do it. She *hates* having to help her mom in the garden. It's true, I wouldn't dream of helping my parents do something like raking leaves, mainly because I can't imagine either of my parents picking up a rake, even if Dad says he used to when he was a boy. He's always going on about his deprived childhood in Brooklyn and tells us how spoiled we are. I guess that means I'll have to confess to the Deadly Sin of sloth again. *Sigh*.

Mac, Sean, and the twins are in the middle of a game of two-on-two soccer when I step out the back door into the garden. Teresa is in goal. She sees me first.

"Hey, guys, Justine's here," she calls out, giving me a smile and a wave.

Sean uses Teresa's brief moment of inattention to kick the ball past her into the back of the net. He and Mac give each other high fives.

"Sean, you slimeball!" Teresa protests. "That's not fair. I was saying hi to Justine."

"You didn't call for a time-out," Sean says in a superior voice. "That's six–four to Mac and me."

Teresa grabs the ball and throws it at his head.

"You always have to win, even if you have to cheat to do it!" she shouts angrily.

"Hey, calm down, Tee, it's only a game," Tommy says soothingly.

"Well, I'm sick of playing it," Tee shouts, marching into the house.

"Substitution for the Minnesota Twins," Sean announces. "Number sixteen, Justine Silver, in for number eight, Teresa Bad Sport."

"Shut up, Sean," Tommy says irritably. Even though Tee isn't there to get upset, Tommy still sticks up for her. I guess it's a twin thing. I wish I had a twin. It'd be nice to have someone to stick up for me once in a while.

Tommy slaps me five and puts his arm around me so he can whisper instructions in my ear without the others hearing him. I feel the warmth of his arm through my shirt, and it gives me a funny feeling inside. I've never given Tommy much thought before, other than as one of Mac's brothers, but all of a sudden I'm hit by the realization that he is really, *really* cute. He smells great, a mixture of shampoo, soap, and sweaty boy. I silently hope he'll take his time discussing strategy so his arm stays around me for longer. Is this what they mean by lust? I guess Father Ted will have to check off another box on the Sin List.

"You take on Mac and I'll cover Sean," he says in an undertone. "The minute you see them moving toward our goal, get your butt into it and play goalie, okay?"

I nod nervously. I happen to like soccer, but I didn't start at the age of five like the McAllisters did. I think Tommy started kicking the ball around with Sean and Joseph as soon as he could walk. And before that, his older brothers probably used him as the ball when their mother wasn't watching.

Sean throws the ball up in the air, and he and Tommy leap up to head it. Sean gets there first because he has about five inches on Tommy, so the ball heads toward me. I follow Tommy's instructions and get my butt in goal as the three of them come racing down the grass. Tommy is trying all means, fair or foul, to get the ball, but Sean and Mac are pretty good at passing it between them. I see Sean aiming at the goal, and the ball comes hurtling toward me. I dive across the ground, and although I mean to catch the ball with my hands, I miss and it hits me right in the chest.

Now, I'll admit I don't have the biggest chest in the world, but what little I have is screaming in pain. Tommy is punching his fist in the air, shouting, "Right on, Justine!" but I'm finding it hard to revel in my moment of glory because I'm trying to figure out how to hug my arms over my chest without letting the boys know that I'm in pain there.

Mac comes over to give me a hand up.

"Are you okay?" she says in an undertone so her brothers don't hear. Mac's a girl. She understands.

"Yeah," I gasp.

She giggles. "It was a great save. But normally goalies use their *hands.* That's one of the main advantages of being goalie. Being able to use your *hands.*"

"Mac," I say, feeling my face flush.

"What?"

"Shut up, will you?"

She runs back up the field, laughing.

We play for half an hour, by which time I'm hot and sweaty and can barely breathe. I wonder if I'm getting Mom's asthma or if it's just that I'm out of shape.

Mac and I grab some lemonade from the refrigerator and flop out on the trampoline. We lie on our backs, looking up at the sky through bare branches that are just starting to bud. It's one of those late winter days where the sky is a clear, bright blue and it's just the right kind of cold.

Tommy and Sean, who seem to have endless energy for anything to do with sports, have exchanged the soccer ball for a basketball and are shooting hoops in the driveway. I can hear the thump of basketball against the asphalt followed by a reverberating thud when one of them scores.

"How do you think I'd look with a perm?" Mac asks.

I can't believe my ears. Mac has the kind of hair that I would die for. Fine, blond, and best of all, straight. I sit up and stare at her.

"Are you *nuts?*" I exclaim incredulously. "I'd give anything to have straight hair like yours. Why on earth would you want to mess it up with a perm?"

"Because I hate my hair," she says. "It's so . . . flat. You're lucky. Yours is so thick and bouncy."

Thick and bouncy. I never thought of my hair that way. To me it's just frizzy and unmanageable.

"So what do you think about the perm?" Mac asks again. She can be pretty persistent when she wants to be. Maybe because she's the youngest of six. I bet it's all-out war trying to make yourself heard at the McAllisters' dinner table. I mean no one in my family ever listens to *me,* and that's with a lot less competition.

I try to imagine Mac with curly hair. It doesn't compute. To me, she looks perfect the way she is. I tell her so.

"I bet you're just saying that because you're my best friend," she says with a sigh.

It still gives me a warm feeling when Mac calls me her best friend. I wonder if I'll ever figure out what she sees in me.

"No way, José. It's true."

Patches jumps onto the trampoline and settles herself between us, purring loudly. We take turns stroking her soft fur, and her purring grows so loud it feels like the trampoline is vibrating.

I start thinking about going to church with the McAllisters the next day. It makes me excited and nervous at the same time.

"Do you like being Catholic?" I blurt out before I can stop myself.

As soon as the words are out of my mouth, I wish I could take them back. Mac's going to think I'm weird for asking a question like that.

But it doesn't seem to freak her out. "Do I like being Catholic?" she says. "I guess so. I mean, I can't imagine being anything different. It's just what I am. What we've always been."

Patches rumbles away between us.

"So what about you?" Mac asks, lobbing the question back at me. "Do you like being Jewish?"

I haven't told Mac that I've given up being Jewish for Lent. For some reason I just can't bring myself to do it.

"Uh, yeah, I guess," I mumble. "But it'd be cool to go to confession like you do."

"Seriously?" Mac sounds genuinely amazed. "I hate going

to confession. I get claustrophobic in the confessional. It's like being in a dark closet."

I feel myself blushing as I think of Father Ted, my big old stuffed bear, and what we do in *my* closet.

But Mac doesn't notice because she's still talking. "I always used to be scared that I'd forget to confess something and then die in a car crash on the way home from church and end up in purgatory."

I, on the other hand, have never given purgatory much thought, because in Judaism the focus is more on how you behave in life than on what happens to you after death. I suddenly think about how I lied to Mac, my best friend, about her silver cross necklace and wonder if I'm going to end up in purgatory, or even worse, hell. It's a scary thought.

Mac and Teresa share a bedroom. I guess when you have six kids you have to double up. You can tell which is Mac's side and which is Teresa's. Teresa has pictures of cute movie and TV stars wallpapering the space around her bed. Mac has posters of her favorite women's soccer team.

I can't imagine having to share a room with Helena. Maybe that's what will happen to me in purgatory—I'll be stuck sharing a room with my snotty older sister for all of eternity. That would be punishment all right.

Despite numerous warnings from Mr. and Mrs. McAllister that the three of us should be quiet and go to sleep, we stay up well past midnight painting one another's nails, making up stories, and listing the boys we think are hot, in increasing order of hotness. Thankfully, the fact that I have developed a huge crush on Tommy seems to have escaped his sisters' notice, and I make sure not to include him on any of my lists. Some secrets are way too embarrassing to share, even with your best friend.

Mrs. McAllister has to work hard to get us up the next morning.

"If you want a cooked breakfast, you'd better come down right now, because my breakfast shift is nearly over," she says, before moving on to wake up Sean and Tommy.

Mac and Teresa would probably be happy to sleep in and have a bowl of cereal, but I'm not about to miss the opportunity to have one of Mrs. McAllister's breakfasts. So after I carefully brush my hair and try to arrange it so it looks presentable (I don't want to bump into Tommy in the hallway with "fun hair"), I drag the two of them out of bed.

It's worth it. Mrs. McAllister makes us blueberry pancakes, and they're great—fluffy with a dab of butter melting in the middle. We don't even *have* butter in *our* fridge—*fat* is a four-letter word in the Silver household.

Sean walks in, followed closely by Tommy, just as I'm finishing up my first pancake. Tommy looks unbearably cute in flannel pajama bottoms and a faded Yankees T-shirt. My face feels hot, and I hope that nobody notices I'm blushing. Especially Tommy. I keep sneaking looks at him as I eat my second pancake, although for some reason I'm not as hungry for it as I was before he sat down across the table from me.

"I'm glad I didn't give up your pancakes for Lent, Mom," Sean says, taking a swig of orange juice.

"What did you give up?" I ask curiously.

"Well, it obviously wasn't being a jerk," Teresa says sarcastically. She clearly hasn't forgiven him for yesterday.

"That's enough, Teresa!" warns Mrs. McAllister, who is busy unloading the dishwasher.

"Actually, it was chocolate," Sean says loftily.

Chocolate seems to be a popular choice for Lenten denial. This is something I find hard to understand. I can't go more than twelve hours without chocolate. And that's the twelve hours when I'm sleeping.

"I gave up buying new clothes," Teresa says. "And I'm donating the money I would have spent to the Catholic Aid drive."

"That's so great," I tell her, genuinely impressed by her charitable act. I wonder if I can get Mom to give me the chicken I would have eaten if it weren't Lent to donate to the local soup kitchen.

"With the amount of money you spend on clothes, they should be able to feed a small country in Africa," Tommy jokes.

"Well, I don't think giving up MTV watching is all that impressive," Teresa snaps tartly. "Unless you spent that time volunteering to help people or doing something useful for a change."

"Giving up MTV for six weeks is a big sacrifice when you are as plugged into the musical scene as I am," Tommy protests. "It's hard work being the King of Cool."

Something suspiciously like a snort comes from the direction of the dishwasher.

Tommy studiously ignores his mom and turns his attention to me. His eyes are even bluer than Mac's.

"So what have you given up, Justine?" he asks.

"She's Jewish, you idiot," Mac interjects. "She doesn't have to give up anything."

"Actually, I've given up being Jewish for Lent," I say, in what I hope is a breezy, casual manner.

I realize I haven't achieved it when four sets of blue eyes stare at me from around the table. There is an awkward moment of shocked silence.

"Now why would you want to do that, Justine?" Mrs. McAllister asks gently, leaving the dishwasher to come sit at the table. "Debbie, one of my best friends from college, is Jewish. I used to wish I were, too."

Wild. I never imagined anyone would *want* to be Jewish. Wanting to be one of the people everyone else seems to hate. Our rabbi made a joke about how most Jewish holidays can be summed up by "They tried to kill us, we survived, now let's eat." I mean, look what happened to Bubbe and Zayde's families.

"But . . . why?" I can't help asking.

"Oh, lots of reasons," Mrs. McAllister says slowly. "For one, Debbie's family was always so warm and loving. So *involved*. They were really interested in what she was learning. I went to stay with them one weekend, and after their Sabbath meal they sat around the table for hours talking about the things we were learning, current events, and arguing about intellectual points just for the sake of it. Debbie said that discussion and debate was encouraged when she went to Hebrew school. Apparently that's the way Jews have been taught throughout the ages."

She pauses and gives me a wry smile. "My family wasn't like that. We were all too busy eating, and then when the meal was finished we just did the dishes and watched TV. Or sometimes some of us would play board games. But with ten children, there was always some chore that needed doing. My mother didn't have the energy to sit around and argue politics or the existence of God. The minute dinner was over she was folding laundry, ironing, or doing the lunch boxes. She believed in the Father, the Son, and the Holy Spirit, and that was that. And we were expected to do the same, no questions asked."

Okay, so Mrs. McAllister's friend's parents actually *talked* to their children. I know that's pretty unusual. Most parents talk *at* their kids. Still. I mean, that doesn't seem to have anything to do with being Jewish or Catholic. This Debbie's family sounds more like the McAllisters than the Silvers.

"But being Jewish is all about suffering," I argue. "People hate us, try to kill us, and don't want us to join their country club, while you guys get Christmas trees and Easter eggs."

There are giggles from around the table, but Mrs. McAllister is serious.

"All religions have persecution in their history," she says. "Take the Huguenots in France, Catholics in Northern Ireland, Muslims in Bosnia, or the Kurds in Iraq. But your heritage is so rich with tradition."

Sean gives a loud and exaggerated yawn. "Give Justine a break, Mom. Sunday is supposed to be our day off from school."

Mrs. McAllister gives Sean a LOOK. As parental looks go, hers is pretty impressive. It would shut me up. She leans forward and takes my hand.

"Be proud of where you come from, Justine." Mrs. McAllister says. "If you aren't happy with who you are, then the grass will always look greener somewhere else. But when you get there you won't be any happier, because you've taken your insecurities with you."

Everyone's looking at me, and I can feel myself blushing again. I'm relieved when Mrs. McAllister looks up at the clock and says, "Good heavens! Look at the time! Come on, guys, clear the table and run and get dressed, or we'll be late for mass."

Phew! Saved by the bell. But as I head upstairs with Mac and Teresa, I hear Mrs. McAllister's words about being happy with who I am spinning around and around in my head.

Chapter Four

I walk into St. Bernadette's Church surrounded by the McAllisters. I'm hoping that I just blend in with the scenery. I'm half expecting a thunderbolt to come down from heaven to strike me dead as I pass through the heavy oak doors, although I'm not sure if I'm expecting one from Jesus because I don't say His name when I do my Hail Marys, or from God for being in church and pretending to be Catholic.

Sometimes, I wonder if Jesus, Allah, and God are all the same person. I imagine that J-A-G person sitting up there in heaven, shaking His head with tears in His eyes because He can't understand why His children are fighting and killing one another in His various names, not realizing that they're all praying to the same guy.

I watch each of the McAllisters cross themselves, and do a little knee bend before they slide into the wooden pew. I feel kind of funny not doing it when it's my turn. I slip into the pew next to Mac, and my heart speeds up when I realize Tommy is sliding in behind me. His arm touches mine when

Teresa pushes him to move over from his other side so Mr. and Mrs. McAllister have room to sit down at the end of the row, and my mind starts to fill with all kinds of unchurchlike thoughts. I struggle to think of pure and wholesome things, like I imagine my secret alter ego, Sister Teresa Benedicta, would.

Sister Teresa Benedicta was the only Jewish saint. Well, she wasn't really a Jewish saint, because by the time they made her a saint, she wasn't Jewish anymore. She decided to be an atheist at the age of fourteen, but ended up a Carmelite nun. She was called Edith Stein before she got her Catholic name. She ended up being killed in Auschwitz, the place Bubbe had the numbers tattooed on her arm. I guess to some people, if you are born Jewish it doesn't matter if you've given up being Jewish for Lent, like me, or for good, like Edith Stein. You can even become a nun and be made a saint, but they still think the world is a better place without you. What makes people hate so much?

As I sit in the pew, I wonder if Edith Stein ever practiced being Catholic in the closet when she was my age. Or if she ever felt tingles on her arm when her friend's brother sat next to her in church. Before I could never understand why men and women sit separately in synagogue. Now I know. It's hard to concentrate on pure and heavenly thoughts when you have developed a sudden, overwhelming crush on the guy sitting next to you. I've got to remember to tell Father Ted I'm having problems with the lust thing.

I'm jerked out of my reverie when I notice that everyone around me is down on the floor, kneeling on these little pillow things. Glancing around, I realize that I'm the only one in the entire church with my head above the pew. Uh-oh. I quickly hunch over in the seat. I can't bring myself to kneel, but at least I won't be as conspicuous if the priest looks up to check on his flock. I try as hard as I can to remember the Catholic prayers that are scribbled on that piece of paper hidden in the sock in my closet, but my mind's gone blank except for the guilty thought that I have Mac's cross hidden there, too. Purgatory, here I come.

I figure I might as well be praying something to someone, so I start to whisper in Hebrew: "*Shema Yisrael Adonai Elohainu, Adonai Echad* . . . Hear, O Israel, the Lord is our God, the Lord is One." It's one of the main prayers of Judaism, and saying it makes me feel less out of place, even if I have given up being Jewish for Lent.

I wonder if Edith Stein felt as weird as I feel now when she walked into a church for the first time, or if she had a sudden beam of heavenly light shine down at her through the stained-glass windows, like it does in the movies, and thought, *That's it! I'll become a nun. It's what I was always meant to be.*

I don't feel any divine intervention. I just feel conspicuous and strange. It's so different from what I'm used to, from the melodies of the hymns to the smell of the place, which is heavy and sweet with incense.

At one point, everyone gets up and starts shaking hands with one another and saying "Peace be with you." I'm pretty psyched, thinking that it's all over, because that's what people do at the end of our Sabbath services, except they say it in Hebrew, *"Shabbat shalom."* I turn to move out of the pew just as everyone else sits down, and I end up tripping over Tommy's legs and landing sprawled on the floor on top of his and Teresa's feet.

Purgatory is looking mighty good to me right about now.

My face is so hot from blushing that the flames of hell would feel like air-conditioning. Maybe this is the modern-day equivalent of a thunderbolt. It certainly feels like punishment, because the people in the row in front have turned around to see what caused the ruckus, and all the McAllisters are giggling, even Mr. and Mrs. I crawl backward and slide back up onto the bench between Mac and Tommy, feeling more embarrassed than I ever have in my entire life.

"What on *earth* happened to you?" Mac giggles in my ear.

"I thought it was over after everyone got up and shook hands," I whisper back, feeling my eyes get all prickly like I'm going to cry. "That's what happens at synagogue."

"No, that's just the Peace," whispers Mac. "We still have Communion to go. Don't worry. It's not much longer now. I *told* you you'd be bored."

I struggle to give her a grin. "It's not boring at all," I tell her. "It's interesting. Really."

She gives me that raised-eyebrow thing she does when she wants me to know she thinks I'm crazy, then turns back to her prayer book.

When it's time for Communion, Mac and Sean squeeze past my legs and follow Mr. and Mrs. McAllister, Teresa, and Tommy up to the front of the church, where a whole bunch of people are lined up on their knees. I feel like everyone is looking at me because I'm not taking Communion, until I realize there are several other people scattered around the church who have remained in their seats. Mac told me that you can't take Communion unless you've been to confession, and I look around at the other people trying to imagine what sins they've committed that are so terrible that they can't even confess them to their priest. They all look like such nice, ordinary people, even the guy dressed all in black with spiky, bleached hair and an earring. I can't imagine them doing anything that is unconfessable. I wonder if they are sitting there imagining the bad things *I've* done—other than making a commotion in church, that is.

Finally it's all over. We pile into the McAllisters' minivan and head back to their house. When we get there, I'm surprised to see my mom's car already in the driveway. My dad was supposed to pick me up, and not until after lunch.

Mom and Jake get out of the car the minute they see the McAllisters' car pull into the driveway. I get a funny feeling in the bottom of my stomach when I see the look on Jake's face. He looks, well, scared.

"Hello, Kathy," my mom says to Mrs. McAllister. "I'm sorry we need to pick up Justine a bit early."

She comes over and hugs me. So does Jake. Now I *know* something is wrong.

"Mom, what's going on?" I ask her, feeling more scared by the minute.

Mom hesitates for a second.

"It's Bubbe," she says gently, squeezing my shoulder. "She's had a stroke. Dad and Helena are at the hospital."

I can't seem to move my mouth. It's hard to take in what Mom's just said. Not my Bubbe. It just can't be.

The McAllisters have all gathered around us now, and Mrs. McAllister and Mac pat me on the shoulder sympathetically.

"Is she . . . dead?" I manage to stammer, feeling a sob coming up in my throat. I've always known that Bubbe is old, and not in the best of health, but I've never thought about her dying.

"No, sweetheart. But she's in intensive care," Mom says.

All of a sudden I'm struck by a terrible thought.

"When . . . when did it happen?"

"This morning," Mom says. "Fortunately, Mrs. Schotstein, the lady downstairs, has a key to Bubbe's apartment. She heard a crash and went up to check on her. When she found Bubbe, she called the ambulance right away."

A wave of guilt washes over me, guilt so strong that I feel sick to my stomach and start to cry. Because I know it's my fault. For sitting in church and thinking about how good it felt when Tommy's arm touched mine, committing the Deadly Sin of lust instead of praying and thinking about holier things. But especially for pretending to be Catholic and wanting to go to mass.

When he sees me cry, Jake starts crying, too. So does Mac, and even Tee looks like she is fighting back tears. Through the heavy fog of guilt and misery I wonder why they're crying. I bet *they've* never been so wicked that their grandmother had a stroke as punishment.

"Come on, Jussy, she's going to be fine," Mom says soothingly, although I can tell that she isn't convinced this is the case. "Grandma's a tough old lady. She survived Auschwitz. She won't let a little thing like a stroke get in her way."

"Why don't you all come inside for a cup of tea?" says Mr. McAllister. "I'm sure this has come as a terrible shock."

Mom declines. "We need to get to the hospital," she says. "I know there isn't much traffic this time on a Sunday, but I think Marcus wants us there as soon as possible."

Mr. and Mrs. McAllister nod and murmur in agreement, and I wonder if it's because they think Bubbe might die before we get there.

"Teresa, run upstairs and get Justine's overnight bag," says Mrs. McAllister. She also goes inside and comes out with a few bottles of water and a brown lunch bag.

Wrapping her arms around me, Mrs. McAllister gives me a big hug. "She'll be all right, Justine. We'll all pray for her."

At the mention of praying, I cry even harder. I feel like a twenty-ton weight of guilt is pressing me down. It's so heavy that I know any minute a big hole will appear right under my feet, and I'll be swallowed up with a one-way ticket to a hot and fiery place.

Mrs. McAllister takes a tissue out of her pocket and gives it to me.

"Don't cry, love." She hands me the brown bag. "I've filled it with oatmeal-raisin cookies for you."

Mac and Teresa each give me a hug, and even Tommy and Sean give me a tap on the shoulder before I get in the car.

"Don't worry, your grandmother will be okay," Tommy mutters, but his eyes are focused on a pebble in the driveway when he says it, so I know he's just saying it to make me feel better.

As we pull out of the driveway, I look back at the McAllisters, who are standing by the basketball net, waving. I wish I could go back to this morning, sitting around the breakfast table eating Mrs. McAllister's fluffy pancakes, when my biggest fear was that Tommy would realize that I had a crush on him. I wish that I'd told my parents that I wanted to be picked up early so I could go to Hebrew school, instead of being glad to get out of going and excited because I could go to mass. But most of all I wish God had punished *me,* instead of taking it out on my poor old Bubbe, who's already suffered so much in her life.

It's a quiet, miserable drive into the city. Jake and I don't fight once, a sure sign that things are not as they should be. We hardly even talk, each of us lost in our own thoughts, and I don't touch the cookies that Mrs. McAllister gave me, despite the fact that I haven't had lunch and they're my favorite.

Suddenly Mom's cell phone rings. It sounds ten times louder than usual. My stomach churns as Mom puts on her earpiece and answers the phone. I imagine the worst. I keep trying to remember when I last told Bubbe how much I love her, or if I ever told her that she's the only one in my family who understands me.

Mom's going "Um . . . Yes . . . What did the doctor say? . . . No. We're on the Hutchinson River Parkway, about Pelham . . .

I'd say about another twenty minutes, plus however long it takes us to park . . . Okay . . . See you soon."

The minute she hangs up Jake and I both ask, "What happened?" at the same time and we don't even say "Jinx."

"That was Helena. Bubbe's still in intensive care, but at least she's conscious now," Mom says.

I sense that Jake, like me, is breathing a sigh of relief that Bubbe is still with us. We sink back into silence, into our private worlds of worry.

When we get to the hospital, Mom, Jake, and I have to wait outside the intensive-care unit while one of the nurses goes in to bring out Helena, because Bubbe is only allowed two visitors at a time. Mom warns Jake and me to behave ourselves and stay put. Jake takes his Game Boy out of his pocket and tries to lose himself in a game. The stupid music drives me crazy, but I'm too tired and miserable to start a fight.

The doors to intensive care swing open, and Helena comes out, looking pale and even thinner than usual. As soon as she sees Mom, she throws her arms around her neck and starts to cry.

"What is it? What's happened?" I ask anxiously.

Helena is sniffling, and the nurse behind the desk at the door of the ICU silently holds out a box of tissues. After blowing her nose loudly at least five times, Helena finally says, "She looks so frail," in a shaky voice. "But they say that she's a lot better than she was when she first came in."

"Do they say anything about her prognosis?" Mom asks worriedly.

"It's too early to say." Helena sniffs.

"I'm going in," Mom says grimly. After giving Jake and me another warning to behave, she disappears behind the frosted-glass doors.

Helena sinks into a chair. I sit down next to her and start shooting questions. "How is she? Is she going to be okay? How does she look?"

"I don't know if she's going to be all right!" wails Helena. "And she looks *terrible!*"

She puts her face in her hands as if she wants to shut out the image of Bubbe in the hospital bed. Jake and I exchange terrified glances, and then he loses himself back in his Game Boy. I wish I had a book to read, because the only magazines they have in the ICU waiting room are *Car and Driver,* five-year-old copies of *Highlights for Children,* and a few tattered *Reader's Digests.* By the time Mom comes out, I've read all the *Reader's Digests* and am about to start on the *Highlights,* even though they're way too babyish for me, just so I don't have to think about what might be happening behind the frosted-glass doors.

I'm the first one to get to Mom after she emerges. "So how is she?" I say, grabbing her hand for reassurance.

"Well, she's conscious and she can understand what we're saying," Mom says. "But her speech is slow and slurred."

With an obvious effort, Mom pastes on a bright smile. "Still, the doctor is hopeful that she will make almost a full recovery."

That's good news, I think. "So is it my turn to go in now?" I ask, desperate to hold Bubbe's hand and to see for myself that she is still there.

Mom gives my hand a squeeze. "I'm sorry, Jussy, but children under the age of sixteen aren't allowed in intensive care," she says gently. "You and Jake will have to wait out here."

"But that's not fair!" I explode. "Helena got to see her. I want to see her, too!"

Mom tries to reason with me. "Sweetheart, you can't. It's the hospital rules."

I'm in no mood to be reasoned with. I start to cry. "I don't care about the stupid rules! I want to see Bubbe!"

The nurse behind the desk is on the phone, but her arm emerges again from behind the desk, wielding the box of tissues. She must be used to scenes like this. Mom takes a tissue and hands it to me. I grab it from her and blow my nose so hard that it starts to bleed. That's how I feel inside. Like I'm bleeding.

Mom sighs heavily, grabs a few more tissues, and sits me down with my head back while she pinches the tip of my nose to stop the flow.

"Jussy, I know it's hard, but we have to abide by the hospital rules. Hopefully Bubbe will be out of the ICU soon. Then you can visit her all you like."

She dabs at my nose with one of the tissues. "Dad will come out in a minute and take you all down to the cafeteria for some lunch. He needs to eat. And so do you, Helena," she says, eyeing my sister sternly. Helena has this thing about not eating because she thinks she's fat. She and all of her friends think that being anything above a size zero means you are ready for the fat farm. If that's what it takes to be one of the popular girls, you can count me out. I can't see denying myself chocolate just to fit into a smaller pair of jeans. Life without chocolate would be a barren wasteland, like crossing an interminable desert with no oasis in sight. Kind of like what life would be like without Bubbe.

"Right, I'm going in to get Dad," Mom says. "I'll sit with Bubbe while you guys eat."

She goes back inside and the frosted doors slide shut. I'm left outside, unable to enter, fuming at the injustice of a system that lets Helena go in to see our sick Bubbe, but not me.

Chapter Five

After a week in intensive care, Bubbe was moved to a stroke rehabilitation unit in Westchester, and Jake and I are finally allowed to see her. I feel scared as I walk into the hospital, clutching a homemade card and a bunch of purple asters. Bubbe loves asters, because she says they remind her of her village in Hungary.

Mom and Dad visit Bubbe every evening during the week while Jake and I are stuck with Helena babysitting. Luckily, Mrs. Weinstein came to visit one night with Shira and Sammy. She brought homemade chicken soup with matzo balls.

I don't know what it is about Jewish mothers and chicken soup. It's supposed to be a stereotype, but seriously, it's like they believe that eating chicken soup can cure every problem. I wish I could take some of Mrs. Weinstein's soup to my Bubbe. It might not cure her stroke, but I know she always said that Mrs. Weinstein's matzo ball soup was just like *her* Bubbe used to make, so having some might make her feel better. It certainly makes me feel better—that's until I realize that I shouldn't have had any because chicken's one of the things

I've given up for Lent. But I figure Saint Peter, or whoever is in charge of the Lent Police, will forgive me just this once. I mean even on Yom Kippur, the Jewish Day of Atonement when everyone is supposed to fast, people who are sick are allowed to eat and take their medication. Most of the people I know consider chicken soup a form of medication, and I think this situation qualifies as a genuine medical emergency. But just to cover all my bases, I'll put the chicken-soup transgression on the list of things I need to confess to Father Ted.

After dinner, Shira and I go up to my room. Shira doesn't chatter about clothes or boys or nail polish. She tells me what's going on with our friends in New Rochelle, how Jenny Weissman's parents are getting divorced and Ricky Burston's moving to Chicago. I tell her about Mac and some of the other friends I have made here. We commiserate about our bratty younger brothers.

When Bijoux comes into the room, I pick her up and stroke her, something I normally never do. But it feels good to have her warm body cuddled up on my lap, even if she is a useless excuse for a dog most of the time.

Suddenly Shira says, "You know, I really love your Bubbe. I'm sure she's going to be okay."

None of my other friends have told me they love Bubbe. I guess none of my other friends have had a chance to meet her enough to love her. I suddenly wonder if they will ever get that chance, and burst into tears.

Shira puts her arm around me and hugs. "Hey, Jussy, I didn't mean to make you cry." She smiles wryly. "I was actually hoping to make you feel better. I guess I failed miserably."

I let out a little choke of laughter and find myself laughing and crying at the same time. It makes me wonder if I'm losing my marbles. Bijoux squirms in my arms and licks my face with her little pink tongue.

Shira doesn't appear to think I'm crazy. She gives me another hug then gets the box of tissues from my bedside table.

I suddenly think of the card the Weinsteins gave me when we moved away from New Rochelle. Shira wrote out the words to an old Girl Scout song: *Make new friends but keep the old. One is silver, the other gold.* Having Mac as my best friend is great, I love Mrs. McAllister, and I can't stop thinking about Tommy and the way my stomach seems to do somersaults when he is near me. But there's something really comforting about being with Shira. Maybe it's because she's so familiar. I mean we've been friends since before we were even born. Our moms met at Lamaze class.

I've just about got myself all cried out when Mrs. Weinstein comes in, carrying a tray with three mugs of hot chocolate and a plate of cookies.

"I thought we could all use a little treat," she says.

"We're not allowed to eat in our rooms," I tell her hastily. "Or drink anything except water. Mom will flip out if we spill anything on the new carpets."

I don't want Mrs. Weinstein to get into trouble with Mom. "She gets really uptight about stuff like that," I explain, and then, because I don't want it to sound like I'm being mean about Mom, I add, "You know, what with it being a new house and all," even though Mom was pretty uptight about stuff like that in the old house, too. She's just gotten worse, that's all.

Mrs. Weinstein puts the tray down on my desk and comes to sit next to me on the bed. She puts her arm around me and touches my cheek where the remains of my tears have dried on my face. I probably look like Dracula's mother-in-law because my eyes are so red from all the crying I've done since last Sunday.

"You let me worry about that, sweetheart," Mrs. Weinstein says kindly. "I don't think Adele will mind us breaking the rules just this once."

We each take a mug of hot chocolate and a cookie, and sit on my bed to enjoy our illicit treat. Even Bijoux has a cookie, so she doesn't feel left out. She's just one of the girls tonight.

There aren't that many of my friends' moms with whom I can imagine sitting around on my bed having hot chocolate and cookies. I can't even imagine doing it with *my* mom, because I'd be so worried about spilling my drink or getting crumbs on the bedspread. But it seems cozy and natural doing it with Mrs. Weinstein and Shira. We talk about people in New Rochelle, even about Bubbe. For the first time all week I don't cry when I talk about her, and even begin to believe that she'll get better, because Mrs. Weinstein and Shira seem so confident that God is looking out for her.

But I'm still scared as we take the elevator up to the third floor of the Finkelstein Rehabilitation Center. All these questions are running through my head, but I'm afraid to ask Mom and Dad because they don't look like they're in the mood for answering. I wonder if Bubbe looks different. Will she remember me? Will she be able to understand what I say and be able to answer me?

Mom and Dad lead the way down the long hallway with doors opening into patients' rooms. It smells funny, like the stuff the janitor uses to wash the floors in the cafeteria. Some people in the beds are just lying there, not reading or talking or watching TV, just staring into space. It's scary.

When we get to Room 302 I see someone waving to us, and I realize it's Bubbe. I fling my arms around her neck and start to cry.

I feel her hand come up to stroke my hair.

"Come now, *mammele,* what's with the tears? Your old

Bubbe is still here," she says, but she sounds like she does when she's had the fourth cup of wine at the Passover seder, slurring her words. I guess that's because of the stroke.

By this time, Jake, Helena, and my parents have made it to the bed, and Bubbe hugs all of them in turn. I give her the asters, and her eyes light up.

"What a thoughtful child you are, remembering your old Bubbe's favorite flower," she says. "Marcus, can you ask the nurse for a vase so I can have these on my bedside table?" she says to Dad.

Her bedside table is already crowded with the cards that Jake, Helena, and I made for her. There are two other vases of flowers, but none of them are purple asters. I feel proud that I'm the only one who remembered that they're her favorite.

While everyone is talking I sit on the bed next to Bubbe, holding tight to her cold hand, and look at her. She looks the same but different; older, more frail, and even though this is probably impossible, smaller. The left side of her mouth is turned down, even when she smiles. But her blue eyes still twinkle when she looks around at us, her family.

When Dad gets back with the vase, I reluctantly let go of Bubbe's hand so I can arrange the flowers in it. I put the vase on the tray table that goes across the foot of her bed so she doesn't have to twist her head to see them.

"How beautiful they are, Jussy," she says, smiling in that strange, lopsided way. "They remind me of our garden in the old country."

"Now, Ma, when the doctor gives the okay for you to be discharged, you'll move in with us for a while," Dad says firmly.

"Marcus, we talked about this," Bubbe says wearily. "I want to go back to my apartment."

"But how on earth will you look after yourself?" Mom asks.

"I'll get help," Bubbe says. "Mrs. Schotstein knows someone. And she's always downstairs."

"But, Ma, that's crazy," Dad protests. "First of all, it'll cost you a fortune to have round-the-clock help, and you can't rely on Mrs. Schotstein to be home all the time."

Bubbe opens her mouth to argue, but I squeeze her hand until she looks at me.

"*Please*, Bubbe," I beg, tears starting to well up again. "Please come and stay with us."

"Yeah, stay with us, Bubbe," Jake pleads. "We'll look after you. We promise."

Bubbe's eyes get all watery, and she looks up at Dad helplessly.

"How can I possibly refuse when they ask so nicely?" she says with a quaver in her voice.

Jake and I hug her, tight.

"*Oy vey,* not so tight!" Bubbe exclaims. "You'll break poor old Bubbe's bones!"

But she is smiling, that strange, crooked stroke smile, even though it looks like she has tears in her eyes.

Bubbe is in the stroke unit for another two weeks. Mom and Dad go to visit her every day, Dad before work, and Mom while we're at school. We only get to go on the weekend, even though I keep pleading to go during the week. But Mom says that she is too tired to keep schlepping back and forth, and besides, we have homework to do. I think it's mostly because she's worried about Bijoux, who mopes when Mom is away a lot. It makes me mad that her stupid dog is more important to her than me visiting Bubbe.

One day, when Jake and I get home from the bus stop, Helena meets us at the door. She's gotten really unbearable since this all happened. It's like she thinks she's been elected boss over Jake and me because she was old enough to go into intensive care and we weren't.

"Mom called to say she's stuck in traffic because there's been a bad accident on the parkway," she says, brimming with self-importance. "She said that I'm in charge till she gets back, and that you're to get on with your homework."

I hate when Mom puts Helena in charge. She's only five

years older than me, for heaven's sake. So I do the one thing that I know is guaranteed to make her mad, and that's ignore her. It gets her really steamed up.

But Helena knows how to hurt me back. She waits until I've got myself a glass of water and grabbed a chocolate bar to sneak upstairs to my room then says in this fake nicey-nicey voice she uses when she's trying to imitate Mom, "Are you sure you really NEED that chocolate, Jussy? Remember, a moment on the lips, a lifetime on the hips."

I see red. Well, pink actually, because I can feel myself starting to cry, so the red is getting diluted. I'm sick of the way the women in my family—well, except for Bubbe—nag me about my weight. It's like they think it's the defining part of me. It's not my fault I inherited the short, fat, and dumpy genes. And just because Saint Helena takes after Mom and Grandma Lila and got to be tall and skinny, she doesn't have to make me feel bad about eating chocolate. Everyone with half a brain knows chocolate is the Elixir of Life.

So even though I know that my mom thinks I'm overweight and that eating two chocolate bars will make me feel too sick and full to eat the healthy stuff at dinner, I grab a second chocolate bar just to spite Helena, stick my tongue out at her, then go up to my room to tackle my homework.

Bijoux is moping around outside my parents' bedroom feeling sorry for herself. Since I'm feeling pretty sorry for myself, I figure that we actually have something in common. So I let her follow me into my bedroom, then slam the door as hard as I can. I know it's stupid and immature, but it makes me feel better.

I get out my homework, sprawl out on the bed, and open the first bar of chocolate. I eat the first bar and a half so quickly I barely taste it. Then I see Bijoux's sad brown eyes peering at me from the side of the bed. Even though she's pretty annoying most of the time, she looks so miserable I lift her onto my bed (rule-breaking alert number one) then give her a piece of chocolate (rule-breaking alert number two). She snuggles up next to me as I do my homework, and I alternate between eating squares of chocolate myself and giving a square to Bijoux. I figure it's a way of dieting, because I'm only eating half the chocolate, even if I did take two chocolate bars to begin with, so I'm probably eating the same amount as I would have in the first place. But it *feels* like less when I share it with Bijoux, and I'm not as lonely with her curled up next to me on the bed.

I wake up early the next day. It's impossible to stay asleep because Mom's screaming. I jump out of bed and run to my parents' room, convinced that Dad's had a heart attack or something. But when I get there, closely followed by Helena and a sleepy-eyed Jake, I find Mom clutching Bijoux wrapped up in a large bath towel, and pointing hysterically at a series of gross-looking brown patches on the custom-made duvet.

"Marcus, wake up!" Mom's screaming at Dad, whose snores are audible from beneath the pillow he's clutching over his head to block out the noise. "Call the vet! I think my baby is dying!"

"Hey, let me see!" exclaims Jake, who is suddenly wide-awake at the prospect of a dead animal to examine. *Boys.*

But Mom won't let him near her precious bundle. "Marcus!" she screams even louder. "Wake up! I need your help!"

Dad slowly removes the pillow and rolls over. Unfortunately, his hand ends up in one of the gross-looking brown patches on the duvet.

"What the . . . ?" he mutters. He doesn't have his glasses on and he's blind without them, so he brings his hand close to his face to see what it is. The smell hits him before his hand gets into focus.

"Who threw up on the bed?" he says in disgust.

"Bijoux!" shouts Mom. "Haven't you been listening to me? We need to call the vet right away!"

By this time Dad has retrieved his glasses from the nightstand and is surveying the devastation on the duvet.

"You made me spend three thousand dollars on a duvet, and now it's covered in puke?" Dad asks in horrified disbelief.

"All you ever think about is money, money, money!" Mom

shouts angrily. "Poor Bijoux is dying, and all you can think about is money!"

It's scary to see my parents fighting like this. I mean, it's not the first time they've fought, but usually it's something we hear through closed doors, not up close and personal. The fighting's worse since we moved; it's usually about the money Mom's spending with Armando and Marcel.

"I'll call the vet," I say nervously, hoping to distract them. "Helena, why don't you get some paper towels to clean up the puke?"

"No way," Helena says, sticking her nose up in the air. "I'll throw up if I have to go anywhere near it. *I'll* call the vet, and *you* can clean up the puke."

Before I can argue with her, she's halfway down the hall, and there's no way Jake's going to do it because despite having lived through the sixties and all that women's-lib stuff, Dad lets Jake get away with no housework because he's a boy. So I get stuck cleaning up the puke. *Figures.*

Mom and Dad have gone downstairs—to speak to the vet in Mom's case and to drink a vat of coffee in Dad's. I get some paper towels and the stain-remover spray bottle. After wiping as much as I can off the duvet with the towels, I spray the duvet liberally with stain remover. At least it doesn't smell as bad afterward, although there are still large brown stains. I can't help wondering if it has something to do with the chocolate

Bijoux and I shared last night, but decide it's more than my life is worth to mention it to anyone.

By the time we get home from school, the vet has examined Bijoux and said that she had a very bad stomachache from eating something she shouldn't. Mom interrogates us as she prepares the rice-and-boiled-chicken dinner that the vet prescribed for Bijoux, to determine who gave her the contraband substance. We all plead innocent, although I know as usual I'm the one that's guilty.

While I'm supposed to be doing research for my history project on the Internet, I type "dog eat chocolate" into a search engine. I learn that while the worst that chocolate can do to a human is to add a few inches to the hips (does this Web site sound like Grandma Lila, or what?), it can be poisonous for dogs. The high fat content makes them barf and have diarrhea, but that's not the worst of it. Apparently, chocolate contains caffeine and bromine, which affect the central nervous system and the heart muscle. The dog gets really hyper and can even die of a seizure.

Wow. Poor Bijoux. I nearly caused her Death by Chocolate. I suppose if you have to die, Death by Chocolate would be the way to go. But I still feel bad, even if Bijoux *is* a useless excuse for a dog most of the time. Plus, I can't imagine what my mother would do to me if I'd killed her precious baby. I'd end up spending the rest of my life in an orphanage in Timbuktu.

After dinner, I get into the closet with Father Ted to confess my transgressions against Bijoux and to pray for Bubbe to get better. I notice there are a lot of matzo crumbs on the floor and spend a few minutes picking them out of the carpet. When I take a matzo out of the box it looks like someone has nibbled on the edges. Maybe Bijoux's been sneaking into my closet for snacks, although I thought I'd been keeping the door shut.

It's hard to remember because I haven't used my closet confessional since the Sunday Bubbe had her stroke. I still can't help wondering if the stroke was God's way of punishing me for going to church with the McAllisters. I'm also confused about what I should pray and, more importantly, to whom I should pray. I mean, I know that I've given up being Jewish for Lent, but I feel funny praying to Jesus to help Bubbe, because *she* hasn't. So sometimes I slip the *Shema* into the rosary, saying it instead of some of the Hail Marys. I figure Jesus won't mind because He was Jewish before He became a Christian.

The day Bubbe is let out of the rehab center, Mrs. Weinstein, Shira, and Sammy come over to stay with us while Mom and Dad go to pick her up. We sit at the kitchen table and make welcome-home signs for Bubbe. Except Helena, that is. She thinks drawing signs is too babyish. She's up in her room painting her fingernails the latest fashionable shade of lilac, and talking nonstop on the phone to her friends and some boy named Zack, who seems to be calling her at least twice a day. You'd think the guy would have better things to do.

Shira and I arrange the welcome-home signs in the downstairs guest room, where Bubbe's going to stay. I asked Mom to get some more purple asters, but she said she didn't have the time to buy them. So Shira and I go into the garden with a pair of scissors and cut some of the daffodils that started lifting their cheerful yellow heads while Bubbe was in the hospital. Mrs. Weinstein finds one of my mom's crystal vases, and we put it on the bedside table. I want everything to be perfect for when Bubbe gets here, because I want her to stay at our house forever. I'm afraid that if she goes back to her apartment, something will happen to her. What if Mrs. Schotstein isn't there to call 911? What if we were just lucky this time, and next time Bubbe dies? I can't imagine the world without her in it.

Just after lunch, Bijoux starts yapping and we see Dad's car pull up in the driveway. We all run outside to welcome Bubbe, who is waving at us from the backseat. Her face is pale, but she's smiling.

Dad opens the trunk and takes out a wheelchair. He

swears a few times trying to set it up—Dad's really smart, but he's not so handy with mechanical stuff. Finally he gets it up and running, and wheels it over to Bubbe's car door.

It's scary to see Bubbe having to be helped into a wheelchair. It's scary to see Bubbe in a wheelchair at all. All of a sudden she seems very frail, like a strong wind might blow her up to heaven. I feel like flinging my arms around her and holding tight, so she has to stay here with me on earth.

Bubbe loves the welcome-home signs and the daffodils.

"So cheerful they are," she says with that strange, lopsided stroke smile. "It makes me feel like summer is right around the corner."

Suddenly she looks sad and tired, and I wonder if she is thinking what I am thinking: *Will she still be here to see the flowers this summer?* I throw my arms around her.

Normally, Bubbe would say something like "*Oy vey*, Jussy, you'll break poor Bubbe's bones!" But this time she doesn't say anything. She just puts her thin arms around me and hugs back, gently stroking the frizzy hair I hate so much back from my forehead.

Mom walks in carrying Bijoux, who seems to have recovered from her Near Death by Chocolate.

"Kids, I think Bubbe should rest for a while," she says. "Let's go into the kitchen and have some cookies."

Right, Mom. Like that's going to make me feel better. I

wish Mom would realize that at almost twelve I'm not a baby anymore, and that this is not something that cookies, even Mrs. McAllister's oatmeal-raisin ones, can make better.

"Do you need anything?" she asks Bubbe. "Do you want me to turn on the TV?"

"No, thank you, dear," Bubbe replies. "I think I'll just rest."

It's weird to see Bubbe so tired and still. She's usually always in motion, either cooking or cleaning. Even when she watches TV she's reading or knitting at the same time. As we file out of the guest room, I look back. Bubbe is lying propped up against the pillows, her eyes already closed. She's so pale and still that she looks like she could be dead.

Oh God, Jesus, Allah, Buddha, or whatever You want me to call You. I'll pray every day, lots of times if You want, if You'll just let Bubbe stay with me.

Chapter Six

Every day when I get home from school, I go in to see Bubbe. She's still spending a lot of the time in bed, and seems constantly tired. I try to ask Mom why Bubbe is still so tired—I mean, it's been almost a month since her stroke, I would have thought she'd be all better by now. Mom explains that Bubbe is an old lady (Thanks, Mom, now tell me something I *don't* know), and when you're old it takes a lot longer to recover from things than when you're my age. She starts to say something about a stroke and then suddenly seems to think better of it.

"What, Mom? What about a stroke?" I ask her.

"Oh, nothing, dear," Mom says. "I can't even remember what I was going to say."

But I can tell she's lying, and the fact that she won't tell me what she was going to say makes me anxious about what she isn't telling me. I wish grown-ups would realize that. I mean they're so worried about trying to protect us kids from knowing scary stuff, they don't seem to realize that we can tell when they're lying, and it makes us even more scared. I end up trying to imagine what it was my mom was about to say, and all I can imagine are terrible things.

To get me off the subject of strokes, Mom tells me I can invite Mac over for a sleepover on Saturday night.

For the next few days I keep hoping that Mrs. McAllister will bring Tommy when she comes to drop Mac off. Though I've been busy imagining terrible things about strokes, I've still managed to fit in a few hours of daydreaming about Tommy's blue eyes and how good it felt when he put his arm around me.

To my great disappointment, when the car pulls up it's only Mac and Mrs. McAllister. I don't mean that the way it sounds, because I'm really psyched to see Mac, but it would have been nice to have a dose of the real Tommy instead of just having to fantasize about him.

Mrs. McAllister's brought a plate of cookies, oatmeal raisin *and* her special chocolate-butterscotch-chip, plus a big bouquet of flowers for Bubbe.

Bubbe felt well enough to get out of bed and walk today. She managed to walk all the way to the family room with her walker, although she was really tired by the time she got there.

Mac and I sit playing S.U.S.A.N. while Mom, Bubbe, and Mrs. McAllister chat. When Mrs. McAllister says that she has to go pick up Sean and Tommy from a soccer match, Mom escorts her to the door.

"Justine, *mammele,*" Bubbe says, "could you be a sweetheart and get the wheelchair to take me back to my room. I'm too tired to walk."

"Sure, Bubbe," I say, jumping up right away. "But don't you want to stay up to eat dinner with us?"

Bubbe smiles, and I notice how pale she looks.

"I would love to eat dinner with you," she says, grabbing my hand and patting it gently. "But I'm feeling very tired."

My face must register my sudden wave of concern, because Bubbe adds quickly, "Maybe after a little rest I'll get up for dinner, okay?"

"That would be great, Mrs. Silver," says Mac, earning herself a smile from Bubbe.

Mac helps me get the wheelchair, and we maneuver it carefully through each doorway, trying not to scratch the paint. Together we lift Bubbe up from the couch and help her into the chair.

"You girls are so strong," she says as she slumps back in the wheelchair. "What I wouldn't give to have half your energy."

Mac and I carefully wheel her back to the guest room. We help her out of the wheelchair and into bed. I sit down next to Bubbe and take her hand.

"Are you sure you're okay, Bubbe? Is there anything I can get for you?" I ask, anxious.

"My sweet, thoughtful girl," Grandma says, squeezing my

hand weakly. "No, I don't need anything, except a kiss and then some rest."

I lean forward and kiss her wrinkled cheek. I've noticed that ever since the stroke she doesn't smell the same. She's worn the same perfume for as long as I can remember, one that smells like roses. I guess since the stroke she hasn't worn it. I have to remember to ask Dad to get it from her apartment. He's going there tomorrow to pick up her jewelry because Bubbe's worried someone might break in to steal it while she's not there.

Mac and I decide to give up on the video games and go outside to shoot a few baskets. I'm not nearly as good at basketball as Mac, but then I don't have a whole crew of older brothers and sisters to practice with. Helena wouldn't dream of shooting hoops with me, because she might break a nail or something. And Jake, although enthusiastic, isn't a whole lot of competition because he's so short.

Mac's getting in five baskets to my every one, but she isn't rubbing it in. She even gives me a few pointers about how I'm shooting. In PE, Mac always makes sure to pick me for her team, even though she knows that I'm not going to be any help in winning. That's what I call true friendship. I always used to be one of the last people picked.

"Your grandmother is so nice," Mac says, breathless after executing a perfect layup.

"I know," I puff, throwing a perfect air ball.

I run to get the ball, which lands with a dull thud in the flower bed behind the basketball net, breaking the stems of a few daffodils. I feel bad to see them lying there, their lives cut short by my lack of skill. But what kind of landscaper is stupid enough to put a flower bed right behind a basketball hoop in the first place?

"She looks better, don't you think?" I ask Mac as I pass her the ball. I'm not sure that Bubbe does look better, but I figure if someone else thinks she does then maybe it will be true.

Uncharacteristically, Mac misses her shot. The ball bounces off the rim. Mac catches it, but instead of shooting again, she holds the ball tightly to her chest and looks at me.

"I guess so," she says slowly. "But this is the first time I've seen her since the . . ."

She hesitates. I guess she doesn't want to say the word *stroke* because she thinks it will upset me.

"Well . . . since she got out of the hospital, so it's kind of hard for me to judge."

It feels like my stomach drops to my feet, and my eyes get all prickly like I'm going to cry.

"Hey, listen, Jussy," Mac says, dropping the ball and coming over to put her arm around me. "What do I know? I'm not a doctor or anything, and like I said, I've only seen her once in the last month. I'm sure she looks better than she did last week, and I bet you anything she'll look even better by next week. My mom told me it takes a while to recover when something like this happens."

"How long did she say?" I ask. "My mom won't even talk to me about it. You're lucky your mom will."

"Your mother probably knows how worried you are and doesn't want to add to it," Mac says diplomatically.

"Yeah, right."

I grab the ball from Mac and shoot. For once, the ball actually goes into the net with a gratifying swish. Persistence obviously pays off. So I decide to persist with my line of questioning, since Mrs. McAllister appears to be more up-front with the medical information than Mom.

"So what did your mom say? How long did she think it would be before Bubbe gets better?" I ask Mac, who is lining up to shoot.

She waits till her ball goes swish through the net before she grabs it and turns to me, looking uneasy.

"She wasn't that specific, Jussy. She just said that recovery from a stroke is a slow and gradual process. I think that's what she said."

Mac turns to shoot again, like she wants to change the subject. I'm kind of disappointed that Mrs. McAllister wasn't more specific. I want exactness. I want a date by which Bubbe will be back to normal and life can be like it was before.

Bubbe's too tired to get up for dinner. Mom makes her a tray, and after I do a lot of begging, she says that Mac and I can have our dinner on trays and eat in the guest room so Bubbe doesn't have to eat all by herself. I can tell Mom's not very happy about us eating in the bedroom. She doesn't trust us not to spill something, and it makes me so nervous that she's nervous that I end up spilling my water all over the carpet. Luckily it's only water, but that's because she wouldn't let me have milk. I guess she knows that besides getting the short, dumpy genes, I inherited the klutz one, too.

"Don't worry so much, *mammele,*" Bubbe says as I'm frantically mopping up the carpet with a wad of tissues from the box on the bedside table, muttering how Mom's going to kill me. "It's only a carpet."

"You don't understand, Bubbe," I say anxiously. "There's no such thing as 'only a carpet' in this house."

Bubbe gives me a tired but knowing smile. "I do understand, sweetheart. But really, it's not so important. When you have kids, you can't have a perfect house. Every stain on the carpet is a sign of life."

Mac giggles.

"We must have the most lively carpets in the whole world," she says. "Mom says she's not going to bother getting new carpets until I've gone to college. And by the time I go to college, she's counting on Patrick being married and giving her grandchildren, and she probably won't want a new carpet with babies around, so I bet we'll have the same disgusting carpet in the family room for another twenty years at least."

Bubbe nods approvingly.

"Your mama is one smart woman," she says. "What's the point of having a perfect house if your whole family is afraid to live in it?"

"You'd better not say that in front of Mom," I tell Bubbe. "That's heresy. You'll be burned at the stake."

We all share a laugh at Mom's expense. I feel kind of guilty laughing with Bubbe about Mom, but I can't help thinking that Bubbe and Mrs. McAllister have the right idea when it comes to this *Better Homes and Gardens* business. I mean, we're all afraid to do anything in this new house, for fear of arousing the Wrath of Mom. Even Dad got yelled at, because he fell asleep watching TV in the family room holding a cup of coffee and spilled it all over himself. Mom wouldn't have minded *that* so much, but he got some on the newly upholstered wing chair. They ended up having a real shout fest, with Mom screaming at Dad that she couldn't even trust him, a grown-up, not to spill things, and how maybe she should buy him a sippy cup. Dad started shouting back how a man couldn't even relax in his own family room without getting an earful, and anyway, he wrote all the checks for her and those *goniff* decorators, so if he wants to spill coffee in the damn family room then she'd better not say anything about it. It was pretty ugly. Mom started crying, and Dad stormed into his office and slammed the door. They made up eventually, thank goodness, because what with all the fighting they've been doing since the move, I've been worrying that they might get divorced.

When we've finished our dinner, with no spillages other than my water, Mac and I kiss Bubbe good night and carry the trays into the kitchen. Jake's mad because he didn't get to eat in Bubbe's room, and I can't help saying in a superior sort of way that it's because he's not old enough to eat without spilling his food. I hear a faint snort from Mac, who's obviously thinking that this is a bit of the old "pot calling the kettle black." I grab her by the arm and make a hasty retreat up to my room before she can reveal my transgression to the rest of the family. I'm not up to facing the Wrath of Mom right now.

We have fun trying on makeup that I "borrowed" from Helena, although I neglect to tell Mac that I did so without asking. I know she wouldn't approve because she's so good. I wish I could be as good as her. As soon as she leaves tomorrow, I need to do some serious confessing.

Mac paints my toenails various shades of purple and pink, and they look really cool, much better than when I do them myself. I usually end up with nail polish all over my feet and on the old towel I'm careful to put on the bedspread to protect it.

I'm in the middle of painting Mac's nails Bubble Gum Pink when she says, "OOOOH! You'll never guess what I found out today!"

I'm never one to shirk from a challenge. I try to guess.

"Um . . . let's see. Mr. Carey"—the overweight football coach—"is really a woman?" I guess. It's the most unlikely possibility I can think of.

Mac bursts out laughing. Luckily, I didn't have the nail-polish brush on her foot, because it's shaking like crazy.

"Justine, you are totally nuts!" she says. "But that's why I like you so much."

"Yeah, well, look at my family. I come from a long line of nutcases, so it's hardly surprising," I tell her wryly.

I have a lot of faults (just ask Helena), but giving up easily isn't one of them, so I try to think of some other possibilities.

"You heard that Mike Chapman"—the most popular, handsome guy in the whole high school—"thinks Helena is ugly and he would rather have all his teeth removed without anesthetic than take her to the prom?" I say wishfully. I realize this hopeful feeling is another thing I'll have to put on the confession list, but I'm feeling it nonetheless.

Mac's foot shakes again when she giggles. It's getting hard to paint her nails properly.

"Oh, you are *sooo* wicked!" She laughs.

She's joking, of course, but her comment stings because I know how many of the sins have been checked off on the list Father Ted's keeping in the closet. Mac doesn't even know the half of it.

"Okay, I give up," I say, starting on her other foot.

"Well . . ." she says, drawing out the suspense, "I just found out today that TOMMY HAS A GIRLFRIEND!"

This terrible, horrible, earth-shattering news makes my hand slip, and I paint a line of Bubble Gum Pink on the top of Mac's foot and across the knee of my jeans where she is resting it.

"Oops!" I say in what I hope is a lighthearted tone, trying not to let Mac know that I have just found out that a world I thought couldn't possibly get worse, just has.

"Who is it?" I ask, even though I know for sure that the answer will make me miserable. My voice sounds a bit strangled, but Mac doesn't notice.

"Athena Johnson," she says. "You know, the cheerleader?"

Sure I know, and I can't believe it. Actually, I can. I just don't want to. Athena Johnson is the antithesis of me—she's tall, blond, and thin, like my sister, Helena. And of course she's a cheerleader. She gets to waltz around school in those short little skirts that show off her long, tanned legs, which seem to remain a perfect shade of golden brown, even in the middle of winter, when my short stubby legs are whiter than those jeans of Helena's that I accidentally washed in bleach.

The Deadly Sin of envy wells up in me with a vengeance. I feel sick to my stomach with it, and from somewhere deep in my brain comes that little voice, the one that always berates me: *Of course Tommy would like someone like Athena Johnson. Why would he like someone as short, fat, and ugly as you, Justine Frieda Silver? And besides, I bet Athena Johnson never borrows her sister's makeup without asking. Athena Johnson is so beautiful she doesn't even need makeup to make her look good.*

That's just the start of it. The more the voice goes on, the sicker I feel, and my eyes start to prickle, which means . . .

"I'll just get the nail-polish remover and some cotton balls to clean off your foot," I say to Mac, fighting back tears. "Back in a sec, okay?"

Without waiting for an answer, I flee the room, run to the bathroom, and lock myself in. Just in time, because I can't hold back the tears for another nanosecond. They come pouring out as I indulge in some hearty, self-pitying sobs. I look at my puffy, red-eyed, tearstained face in the mirror and ask myself why there is so much injustice in the world. Like, why does the one guy I've ever had a crush on have to like someone else? And why does that someone else have to be perfect and gorgeous like Athena Johnson? It's just so unfair. I mean, even her *name* sounds beautiful. I bet there hasn't ever, in the entire history of the world since the Creation, been an ugly person called Athena. As for Justine, well, look at me. I'm Exhibit A.

I'm just resorting to some loud nose blowing when I hear a knock on the door.

"Justine?" Mac says hesitantly. "Are you okay?"

"I've got a stomachache," I lie, hurriedly flushing the toilet to add some credibility to my excuse. "I'll be out in a sec."

"Fine," she says. "You were gone so long I was starting to worry."

I find some of Helena's eyedrops in the medicine cabinet and squeeze a few drops in each eye to get the red out before I go back to my room. Then I grab the nail-polish remover and the bag of cotton balls and head back to face Mac.

She's busy trying to pick the nail polish off the top of her foot.

"Hey, leave it, Mac, I've got the nail-polish remover," I tell her.

Mac looks at me searchingly as I flop onto the bed.

"Are you sure you're okay?" she asks. "You look like you've been crying."

So much for the eyedrops.

"It's just, well, you know, Bubbe," I lie again. The confess-able acts are piling up thick and fast. I'm going to end up spending the rest of my life in the closet at this rate. I bet

Athena Johnson is so good she never has anything to confess. Life is so unfair, and my life is about as unfair as you can get.

"Oh, Jussy," Mac says, throwing her arms around me and patting me on the back. "She'll be okay. I just know she will."

"Yeah," I say, unconvinced, feeling guilty to have used Bubbe as an excuse.

"I'll light a candle for her tomorrow when I go to mass," Mac says. "That's what Mom always does when someone is sick."

Mac's so nice. I don't know why someone as nice as she is wants to be my best friend.

"Thanks, Mac," I say, genuinely grateful, and not just for the candle. "Come on, give me your foot and I'll clean it off, then finish doing your nails."

"Yeah, try to just get my toenails this time," Mac jokes.

Chapter Seven

Mac and I wake up the next morning to the sound of my mother screaming.

"Oh, not again!" I groan, turning over and pulling a pillow over my head to block out the noise.

But Mac doesn't take it lying down. She sits up, reaches over from the bed next to mine, and shakes me.

"Justine, what's the matter with your mom? Shouldn't we see if she's okay?"

I drag the pillow off my head and roll over to face her.

"No way, no how!" I exclaim with bleary-eyed vehemence. "I'm not going to get stuck cleaning up the puke again. Let Helena do it this time."

Mac looks at me like I have finally lived up to my genetic heritage and gone totally wacko.

"What does puke have to do with it?" she asks, getting up to put on her bathrobe. "Come on, Jussy! Wake UP! Your mom is screaming. Something must be the matter."

I can tell Mac is desperate to open the door to see what's

happening, but there's no way I'm going to leave the room and risk getting put on Puke Patrol.

I tell Mac not to worry, that Mom's just screaming because Bijoux's thrown up on her bedspread again.

"She can't possibly be screaming that much because a tiny dog like Bijoux threw up on the bedspread," Mac argues, her brow creased with worry. "My mom would never scream so much about a little bit of puke."

"That's just because your mom wouldn't be crazy enough to spend three thousand dollars on a custom-made bedspread," I tell her.

"That's true," Mac allows. "But still . . ."

Fortunately the screaming stops, but it is replaced by the muffled sound of my parents shouting at each other.

Just then, my bedroom door bursts open and Jake bounds in.

"Hey, Jussy, you'll never guess what happened," he exclaims breathlessly.

I figure it must be something gross, because otherwise Jake wouldn't be so excited.

"Bijoux puked in Dad's water glass, and Dad accidentally drank it before he put his glasses on?" I speculate.

"Justine!" Mac exclaims. "That's *sooooo* disgusting!"

Jake looks at me admiringly. "Wow, Jussy, you have a sick mind."

The sad thing is, from Jake that's a compliment. He leaps onto my bed, narrowly missing my foot when he lands.

"But it wasn't that," he continues, about to burst with excitement. "It was a MOUSE. Mom saw a mouse in her bedroom!"

"A mouse?" I repeat, genuinely amazed. "In the house of the Queen of Clean? Are you sure it wasn't just Bijoux?"

Mac giggles. She's always amazed at how neat my mom keeps our house. And she thinks my hang-up that Mom loves Bijoux more than me is too far-out for words. She asked me once how I could let a little squirt of a dog give me such a complex. She just doesn't understand, because she has the original Dream Mom.

"Of course it wasn't Bijoux, stupid!" Jake says impatiently. "It was a real live furry mouse in her closet."

Both my parents have these enormous walk-in closets, bigger than a lot of apartments in New York City. At least that's what Mrs. Weinstein said when Mom showed her around the house for the first time.

"So did they catch it?" Mac asks.

"Nah," Jake says, obviously disappointed. "I was kind of hoping they would, so I could keep it as a pet. They're going to call an exterminator. I think that's mean."

I can see there's no way I'm going to get back to sleep, and now that the Puke Alert is over, it's safe to leave the bedroom.

Mac, Jake, and I troop downstairs to the kitchen for breakfast. We find Mom shouting into the phone, with the Yellow Pages on the counter in front of her opened to the "Pest Control" section.

". . . and all I can say is, I don't know how you get away with advertising yourself as 'Anytime Anywhere Pest Service' if you aren't open on Sunday!" Mom is yelling at what is obviously the Not Quite Anytime Anywhere Pest Service's answering machine. "I expect you here FIRST THING tomorrow morning, or else I'll be calling the Better Business Bureau to complain about your fraudulent advertising."

She slams down the telephone and turns to Jake and me with an accusing look on her face.

"Have either of you been eating in your bedrooms?" she demands.

"I haven't," Jake protests. Unlike me, Jake hasn't perfected the Art of the Strategic Lie, so I reckon he's genuinely innocent of the charge.

"Neither have I," I tell her. I manage to say this with a straight face because it's almost the truth. The time I ate cookies with Mrs. Weinstein and Shira, Mrs. Weinstein said she would take responsibility, so I don't have to tell Mom about that, and as far as I'm concerned, chocolate, the only other thing I've eaten in my room, isn't food. I eat it solely for medicinal purposes.

"You'd both better be telling me the truth," she warns us grimly. Then, pressing her hand to her left temple, she mutters that she's getting a migraine and sweeps out of the kitchen to go back up to bed, her silk bathrobe flowing behind her like the train on a wedding dress.

If we were at the McAllisters' there would be a great stack of fluffy pancakes waiting on the table for us, and Mrs. McAllister would be waiting to make us more if we were still hungry. But we're at my house. Dad probably rolled over and went back to sleep the minute Mom transferred her fury from him to Not Anytime Anywhere's answering machine, and now Mom's taken to her bed with a migraine without a pancake in sight.

But Mom hasn't entirely left us to starve. She went shopping yesterday. There are plenty of croissants and a yummy-looking coffee cake on the counter, there's cereal in the closet, and milk and orange juice in the fridge.

"What can I get you, Mac?" I ask in my best hostess voice.

"That coffee cake looks yummy. I'll have a piece of that and a glass of orange juice."

"Jake, do you want some coffee cake?" I call out as I cut Mac a big slice.

"Nah, I'll have cereal," comes a faint voice from the pantry, where Jake's checking the cereal boxes to see which one has the best prize inside. We have a strict rule in our house that you're only allowed to get the prize if you eat the cereal. But

Jake emerges from the pantry with his arm buried up to the elbow in a box of Sticky Oaty O's.

"No one is going to want to eat those now that you've stuck your grubby little paw in the box," I tell him. "Anyway, you know the rules. The prize has to fall in your plate when you pour it. You can't just stick your hand in and dig it out."

As usual, Jake ignores me. He finally removes his arm from the box with a Super Ultra Secret Agent Network Decoder Ring clenched in his hand.

"Hey, Jussy, look! I've got a S.U.S.A.N. Decoder Ring," he brags, waving it triumphantly in my face. "You'll never be able to beat me now!"

I'm really jealous. I would kill to have a S.U.S.A.N. Decoder Ring, because there's a password inside that you use to go on the Sticky Oaty O's Web site and get tips on how to beat your opponent in the video game. But there's no way I'm going to give Jake the satisfaction of knowing that I'm green with the Deadly Sin of envy.

"I hate these cereals that have video-game tie-ins," I comment airily to Mac as I pour us each a glass of orange juice. "It's so commercial, and you know what *kids* are like. They see the ad on TV then nag their parents to buy a box when they don't even eat the cereal."

"Buh uh *woo* wike the feareal," protests Jake through a mouthful of Sticky Oaty O's.

"Don't talk with your mouth full, squirt," I say in my best Mom voice.

"Fut up!" Jake mumbles, sticking out his Sticky Oaty O–covered tongue at me.

"Brothers can be *so* gross and immature," I comment to Mac as we sit down with our food at the opposite end of the table from Jake.

"Tell me about it," sympathizes Mac. "I've got four of them."

I feel a sudden pang in the place where I think my heart is as I recall Mac's devastating revelation about Tommy and Athena Johnson. The sharp pang fades to a dull, heavy feeling that lingers over me like a cloud. I feel like someone placed forty copies of *War and Peace* on my heart. And that's the hardcover version, not the paperback.

After breakfast, I put some challah and orange juice on a tray and carefully carry it to Bubbe's room. Mac knocks on the door, but there's no answer. I look at Mac, feeling sick with worry. I'm wondering if Bubbe died in the night and has been lying there alone and dead while I've been busy coveting Jake's S.U.S.A.N. Decoder Ring. I can't remember; is coveting a Ten Commandment sin, or a Deadly Sin, or both?

"Should we open the door to check on her?" Mac whispers. She looks as nervous as I feel.

"Yeah," I whisper back. "I can't believe she's not up yet.

Bubbe's always been an early riser, and she couldn't possibly have slept through Mom's screaming."

Mac opens the door and we creep into the guest room. Bubbe looks so tiny in the queen-size bed, much smaller than she used to. I wonder if people shrink from having a stroke. I'm relieved to hear her snoring softly, but I'm worried because she's still asleep.

I put the tray down on the table, happy that I managed to get all the way across the carpet without spilling the orange juice. Then I go to the bed and sit by Grandma's side.

"Bubbe?" I say softly.

She doesn't wake up.

I shake her gently and say "Bubbe" a bit louder.

She wakes up and looks at me with no recognition, her eyes bleary and unfocused. I'm suddenly scared she's had another stroke and lost her memory. Do strokes do that?

"Bubbe?" I babble nervously. "Are you okay? Mac and I brought you breakfast, challah and orange juice, I hope that's all right but if it isn't tell me and I can get you something else and Mom saw a mouse in her bedroom and I can't believe you didn't wake up because she screamed the house down, didn't you hear her?"

During the course of my monologue, Bubbe's eyes begin to focus, and she gives me a weak smile.

"Justine, *mammele,*" she says, pulling me down to hug her.

"What a wonderful surprise. How nice for your old Bubbe to wake up to your *shayne punim*. And yours, too, Mac."

Mac comes over to the side of the bed and Bubbe squeezes her hand.

"How are you feeling today, Mrs. Silver?" Mac asks her.

Bubbe musters up a smile, but I can tell it's an effort.

"Not so bad, not so bad," she replies tiredly.

"So, Bubbe, didn't you hear Mom screaming before?" I ask.

"No, sweetheart, I didn't," she says. "The pills the doctor gave me, they make me sleep like the dead," she says.

I cringe to hear her say the D-word out loud. Call me superstitious, I don't want her to say it, because if she does, it might happen. I want to throw salt over my shoulder or spit three times—*"Ptuh! Ptuh! Ptuh!"*—to ward off the Evil Eye, but I'm afraid it might upset Bubbe and Mac'll think I'm even weirder than she thought.

"So what was all the screaming about, *mammele?*" Bubbe asks.

"Mom saw a mouse in her closet," I tell her. "She's pretty freaked out."

Mac giggles. "I'll say! Freaked out is an understatement."

Bubbe smiles, and it's a real one this time.

"I can imagine," she says. "So what's the harm of a little mouse? At least it wasn't a rat." She shudders. "I hate rats. In the camps there were rats as big as your mother's dog."

It's a sobering thought, but somehow I don't think it would make Mom feel any better about the mouse.

Mac and I sit with Bubbe until she finishes her breakfast, and then I take the tray back to the kitchen and load everything in the dishwasher. Jake has left all his stuff on the table, as usual. I feel like shouting at him to come back and clean up his own mess, because I know he's probably on the computer, checking out the secret hints he's able to access with the help of his illegally obtained S.U.S.A.N. Decoder Ring. This provokes envy again. I swear it'll be Jake's fault if I end up in purgatory.

But then I think about how I felt when Bubbe wouldn't wake up and I thought she was, well, the D-word. I put Jake's dishes in the dishwasher myself.

The next day when I get home from school, Mom is waiting for me in the kitchen, looking grim. I get a sinking feeling when I see the expression on her face, because it forecasts trouble. I want to get a chocolate bar for moral support, but I know that will only make things worse.

"Hi, Mom," I say in what I hope is a nonchalant manner as I take off my backpack. "How was your day?"

She doesn't answer my question. Not a good sign. She just says, "Justine, please go into the living room. I need to have a serious talk with you. *Now.*"

Uh-oh. Serious talk means serious trouble. Serious talk *in the living room* means *really* serious trouble. If Mom can't deal with this in the kitchen, then I know I'm in deep doo-doo.

I follow her into the living room, trying desperately to figure out which of my many sins I'm going to be asked to account for. I'm relieved when I see that Bubbe is sitting in her wheelchair next to the sofa. She's even better than chocolate for moral support, and a lot less fattening.

I sit down on the couch next to Bubbe, and she gives my hand a squeeze. Mom is pacing up and down in front of the marble fireplace that was imported from some decrepit château in France by Armando and Marcel, her body tense with suppressed rage.

A few seconds pass, which seem like hours to me because I'm waiting for the dam of Mom's anger to burst over my head. She finally turns to me, and my stomach turns over because I know the storm's about to break.

"Well, Justine, the Anytime Anywhere Pest Service finally showed up this morning," she starts off.

"That's good," I reply nervously. "Did they catch the mouse?"

"Not yet," Mom says coldly. "And they think it's more than one mouse. They actually believe we have a NEST of mice in our home."

She shudders visibly at the thought of multiple rodents having the nerve to take up residence in the "Ultimate Showcase of Tasteful Elegance" that she, Marcel, and Armando have created. I can't help thinking that Jake will be pleased because there's a greater chance of catching one to keep as a pet, but I decide not to share this observation with Mom.

"They did a thorough inspection of the house, to try and figure out where the mice are coming from, and how they got into my closet," Mom continues. "And imagine my surprise when they found a bottle of grape juice and an opened box of matzos, not to mention several chocolate wrappers, in YOUR CLOSET!"

This is bad. No, it's more than bad. It's a catastrophe. I've transgressed one of Mom's carved-in-stone commandments: *Thou shalt not eat food upstairs.* Add in the sin of surreptitiously eating chocolate bars when I'm supposed to be watching my weight, and I figure I might as well kiss the rest of my life good-bye. I'm going to be grounded until I'm shuffling around a nursing home.

"Of course I had to thoroughly clean and vacuum your closet so I could disinfect it. There were *mice droppings!*" Mom says, resuming her angry pacing. "And in the course of cleaning, I found THIS."

She grabs something off the mantelpiece and holds it out to me accusingly. To my horror, I see Mac's silver cross dangling from Mom's fingers.

"So, Justine, what is the meaning of this?" Mom demands.

I try to think on my feet even though I'm sitting on the sofa.

"Uh . . . Mac left it here when she slept over," I stammer. It's sort of the truth. But my mom's too smart for me.

"So why was it in your shoe?" she asks. "And please can you explain THIS?"

She holds out a piece of paper, and my heart sinks when I realize it is my carefully written out copy of the Hail Mary.

Jus when I think it can't get any worse, it does.

"And why on earth," Mom continues, "would you be in possession of THIS?"

She holds out the set of rosary beads I'd bought at Revelations.

"Please spare me any nonsense about Mac leaving it here," Mom says angrily. "Because I called Kathy McAllister and asked her if Mac had lost a set of rosary beads. She called back to say that Mac's rosary beads were in a box on her desk."

Mom stops pacing right in front of me. I stare down at the Persian rug ("buy of the century," according to Armando and Marcel) to avoid looking her in the eye.

"I want an explanation, Justine Frieda Silver," she demands. "And I want it *right now.*"

If I had any doubt that I was in seriously major trouble, I certainly don't have it when Mom invokes my horrible middle name in That Voice.

I try as hard as I can to come up with an explanation that

doesn't require me to tell the truth, especially in front of Bubbe. But even I, excuse-thinker-upper extraordinaire that I am, can't think of a way out of this one. I'm forced to come clean.

Bubbe is still holding my hand, and she gives it an encouraging pat. I take a deep breath and go for it.

"I, uh, well, it's like this," I start off, not particularly effectively. I give Bubbe a brief glance, thinking about how much pain I'm about to cause her. It makes me feel sick. She winks at me to show me she's on my side, which only makes me feel worse.

"I decided to give up being Jewish for Lent," I say in a rush. "And chicken. I wanted to be Catholic like Mac. So I bought the rosary to practice with."

"WHAT? GIVEN UP BEING JEWISH FOR LENT? YOU WANT TO BE CATHOLIC?" Mom shouts. "WHAT SORT OF RIDICULOUSNESS IS THIS? HOW CAN YOU DO THIS TO POOR BUBBE, WHO SUFFERED IN AUSCHWITZ JUST BECAUSE SHE WAS JEWISH?"

"There were Catholic people in Auschwitz, too," I protest, before I can stop myself. "Nuns even," I say, thinking of Edith Stein.

But Mom's too angry for a history lesson. It just winds her up even more. She opens her mouth to give me another blast when Bubbe comes to the rescue.

"Adele, leave her," she interjects gently. "It's not such a big thing. All children go through a time of questioning. It's natural. Actually, I think questioning is a sign of intelligence."

Bubbe looks at me, and smiles encouragingly.

"And our Jussy is one smart kid," she says.

Mom's face goes a deep shade of red. I can tell the level of her anger thermometer has just edged up a few more notches. She *hates* when Bubbe defends us to her. She thinks Bubbe is interfering with one of her inalienable rights as a mother, the one that says she can do whatever she likes, even if it's guaranteed to screw up her children for life.

Sometimes, when it happens at the dinner table, I see Mom looking over at Dad, sitting there shoveling food into his mouth like there is no tomorrow, totally oblivious to the simmering family feuds going on around him. You can see her sending a telepathic message to Bubbe that she already had her chance when she screwed up Dad; so now it's Mom's turn to wreak her own brand of devastation on Helena, Jake, and me. Especially me.

"Questioning is one thing, Zofia," Mom says with controlled anger. She's always careful to speak to Bubbe politely. "But hiding religious artifacts in the closet—that's a completely different matter," Mom continues. "And Justine, I would like you to explain why you have an opened box of matzos and a sticky bottle of grape juice in your closet, which had the wonderful effect of attracting MICE into the bedrooms, not to mention staining the carpet in your closet, when you know that food is NOT ALLOWED UPSTAIRS."

I didn't even realize I'd spilled grape juice on the carpet in the closet. If I had, I would have run away to a convent, or at least tried to clean it with some of that foamy carpet-cleaner stuff Mom has in her cleaning arsenal.

Meanwhile, Mom is waiting for my explanation with arms crossed and foot tapping. There's only one thing for it. I take a deep breath.

"Communion," I mutter. "I was practicing Communion."

"Did I hear this right?" Mom shrieks hysterically. "My daughter is practicing COMMUNION in the CLOSET? For this I end up with a NEST OF MICE in the house? What on EARTH were you thinking?"

I sit there, head bowed. I realize that at this point nothing I say will do any good, so the best thing I can do is shut up. That nasty little voice in my head starts up again, telling me what an unlovable loser I am, how I always manage to do everything wrong, that I'm the black sheep of my family. The more it goes on, the worse I feel. I start crying.

"Your father is going to hear about this when he gets home," Mom continues. "He's going to be very upset. Imagine having a daughter who shows such insensitivity to all that his parents suffered in the war!"

That makes me cry even harder, because I already feel

guilty about hurting Bubbe's feelings. It makes me feel worse than the mouse, or even the whole nest of mice, worse than lying to Mac about her silver cross necklace. It's even more painful than knowing I've committed the cardinal sin of staining my carpet with grape juice.

"Adele, leave the child," Bubbe says. "Don't make her feel bad on my account. For me, it doesn't matter. Justine is a good kid. She's an intelligent and inquisitive young lady, doing something that all kids do—questioning her identity."

She strokes my hair gently, passes me a crumpled-up tissue, and whispers, "Don't cry, *mammele.* I'm not upset, and I don't want you to be."

I blow my nose loudly and look up at Mom, teary-eyed.

"I'm really sorry, Mom," I say, in a hiccupy voice. "I didn't mean to stain the carpet, or to attract mice. And Bubbe . . ." I continue tearfully, "I'm so, SO sorry. I didn't mean to hurt you. Really I didn't. You're the last person in the world I'd ever want to hurt."

"I know, Jussy, sweetheart," she murmurs. "Don't cry. You'll make me cry, and that would be a real mess."

Mom notices that Bubbe is looking pale. Her stony face softens a bit. But not much.

"Justine, why don't you take Bubbe back to her room for a rest before dinner. Then you'd better go up to your room to do your homework."

I stand up, sniffing and wiping my eyes with the back of my hand. As I start to wheel Bubbe out of the room, Mom, who is clearly psychic, adds warningly, "And Justine—don't even THINK about hitting the chocolate!"

It's times like this I wonder if my mom hates me, because I can't understand how she can be cruel enough to deny me chocolate when it's plain as the nose on your face that this is one of the times when I need it the most.

Chapter Eight

I spend the evening hiding in my room, only coming out for dinner. Bubbe isn't feeling well enough to come to the table, and because I'm in disgrace I'm not allowed to take a tray in to eat with her. Helena gets to go instead. She flounces past me carrying a plate covered with an assortment of lettuce leaves and carrots, her nose in the air and a superior smile on her face. I want more than anything to stick out my leg and trip her, but figure I'm in enough trouble as it is.

Luckily, Dad is working late, so I don't have to face his disappointment with me on top of the lecture I've already received from Mom. But it's a grim dinner all the same. For once I'm not hungry, even for chocolate. My appetite seems to have disappeared under the weight of Mom's disapproval.

Jake keeps looking at me curiously, and I can tell he's dying to ask questions. I try to subtly shake my head no, because I don't want him to get Mom going again. But subtlety is wasted on Jake. Through a mouthful of mashed potatoes he asks, "So, Jussy, are you Catholic now? Did you really give up being Jewish?"

Mom's fork hits her plate with a clatter, just as my foot comes into contact with Jake's leg under the table, in a less subtle attempt to make him shut up.

"Ow!" he whines, glaring at me.

"Stop it right there, Jake!" Mom says sharply. "It's bad enough that Justine has been so foolish and insensitive. There will be no further discussion of this until Dad gets home from work."

She looks at her watch and mutters angrily under her breath about how Dad is always conveniently working late when there are family crises to be dealt with. Who can blame him? I'd much rather be eating a bar of chocolate or even something healthy like a lettuce leaf alone at my desk than sitting through this silent, painful meal.

"Can I be excused?" I ask quietly.

"Fine," Mom says shortly. "Put your dishes in the sink and go straight back up to your room. No video games."

I was hoping Mom would notice how I'd eaten so much less than usual and be proud of me for something, but disapproval flows from her in silent waves. Sometimes I feel like I'm going to drown in it.

On the way to upstairs, I make an illicit detour to Bubbe's room to say good night. Helena looks annoyed when I come in.

"You're supposed to be going straight up to your room after dinner," she says in her "I'm going to be really annoying and act like your mother" voice. "Mom said. She told me after your little 'talk' in the living room."

I feel tears welling up, but there's no way I'm going to give Helena the satisfaction of seeing them.

"I just wanted to kiss Bubbe good night," I say defensively as I sit on the side of the bed, angry because despite my best efforts, there's a catch in my voice that gives me away.

"And I'm so glad you did," Bubbe says gently, reaching for a tissue and pressing it into my hand as she draws me down for a hug. "Helena, I'm sure your mother didn't mean that Jussy should forgo giving her old Bubbe a hug, no matter how much trouble she's in."

Helena looks miffed that Bubbe is taking my side, and it strikes me how amazingly like Mom she is at times. Maybe that's why Mom loves her so much more than she loves me.

Bubbe gives my hand a squeeze. "It'll be okay, *mammele.* Don't worry."

She gives me a mischievous grin, and her eyes shine with some of their old twinkle. "I'll just remind your father of the time when he came home from college with long hair and those awful pants, what did they call them? Bell-bottoms. He told your Zayde, of blessed memory, that he wanted to be a Buddhist. You should have *heard* the hollering."

I find myself giggling through my tears, trying to imagine

my dad, who is balding and built like an overstuffed teddy bear, sporting bell-bottoms and a ponytail. It feels like a huge weight has lifted from my shoulders. I've been dreading the thought of Dad being mad at me, too.

"Good night, sweetheart," Bubbe says soothingly. "Sleep well, and above all, don't worry. It only gives you wrinkles."

It seems like whatever Bubbe says to Dad works, because the following morning at breakfast, my crimes against family and faith don't come up. Dad even says he'll drive Jake and me to school on his way to the station. We all troop in to kiss Bubbe before we leave. She looks really tired, even more so than usual. But she still manages to give me a wink when I turn to leave.

As I go out the door I overhear Bubbe talking to Dad in a low, urgent tone, something about a Mr. Rothstein and how it must be done today because she isn't getting any younger. I don't understand what it's about. I'm just worried because she sounds stressed.

When I come home from school, Mom won't let me go in to say hi to Bubbe.

"She's got Mr. Rothstein and his secretary with her," Mom says. "Please don't disturb them."

"Who's Mr. Rothstein?" I ask.

"Her lawyer," Mom says abruptly, in the tone of voice that forbids further questioning.

Fortunately, Jake is oblivious to that particular tone of voice.

"Why does she need a lawyer?" he asks. "Is she in trouble or something?"

Hurray for Jake. I was wondering the same thing.

"No, Jake, she isn't in trouble," Mom says wearily.

"So why does she need a lawyer?" Jake persists. "People only get lawyers when they are going to go to jail and stuff."

Helena has been nibbling on a carrot stick while doing her homework at the kitchen table.

"She's doing her will, dummy," she says to Jake. With a sidelong glance at me she adds, "Probably cutting Justine out of it."

I feel a cold chill pass over me, and it's not because Helena's being snotty. I'm used to that. It's because I know that people only do wills when they think they're going to die. Does Bubbe think she's going to die?

My distress must show in my face because for once Mom tells Helena to be quiet and leave me alone. If I weren't so miserable and worried, I'd be happy that Mom finally took my side. But I *am* miserable—and really, *really* worried. I look over at Jake—he looks confused and scared, like maybe he's going to cry.

Mom is busy wiping nonexistent crumbs from the kitchen counter.

"Upstairs now, Jake and Jussy," she says without looking up at us. "Time to do your homework. I'll call you when Bubbe is finished with Mr. Rothstein so you can visit with her."

Jake and I tramp up the stairs, dragging our backpacks behind us. He follows me into my room, sits on the bed, and grabs Father Ted.

"Jussy . . ." he says hesitantly, holding tightly to Father Ted. "Aren't wills for dead people? On TV, people never have a will unless they're dead. Do you think Bubbe is going to . . . die?"

I don't know what to say because I'm scared about the same thing. I mean, I know Bubbe is going to die sometime because she's old and everyone dies eventually, but I always thought it would be when I'm a grown-up, not a kid.

Bijoux wanders in through the open door, and I'm glad for the distraction. I pick her up and hold her warm body against my chest, hoping it will dispel some of the chill I feel in my heart. She licks my face and wags her tail. She's obviously forgiven me for the Near Death by Chocolate incident. Dogs are good like that. They don't bear a grudge the way humans do.

I flop down onto the bed and put Bijoux down next to me. She makes a beeline for my pillow, turns around three times, and curls up in a tiny ball to sleep.

"I don't know, Jake," I finally answer him. "I mean, people

have to be alive when they make their wills, otherwise how would the lawyer know what to write? But . . ."

I don't mean to start crying, but I can't seem to help myself. "I don't want Bubbe to die!" I sniff.

Jake starts throttling Father Ted.

"Neither do I!" he shouts angrily. He throws Father Ted across the room, narrowly missing the lamp on my desk, grabs his backpack, and storms out, slamming the door behind him. But not before I see tears pouring down his cheeks.

Mom calls us down for dinner at six-thirty. I can't believe that Mr. Rothstein has been with Bubbe for such a long time, but it turns out she was so tired when he left that she went straight to sleep.

After dinner, Jake and I finally are allowed to go in to see her. Despite the fact that she just had a nap, she looks exhausted. But she smiles when we come in, and beckons us over to the bed.

"Good evening, *kinderlach*. I'm sorry I missed having dinner with you. Come give your old Bubbe a kiss, my angels."

Jake and I cuddle up on either side of her, and I kiss her pale, wrinkled cheek. We don't talk for a few minutes, but it doesn't seem weird, like it might with some people. It just feels right, and all of a sudden, especially special. I wonder if it takes being afraid of someone dying to realize how desperately you want them to always be there.

As usual, it's Jake who breaks the mood.

"Bubbe, why did you have to make a will?" he asks in a wobbly voice. "Are you planning to die?"

I sit up, lean over Bubbe, and hit him.

"Shush up, Jake!" I hiss, shocked on the one hand that he had the chutzpah to come out and ask the question we'd both been thinking, and admiring him on the other for having the guts to do so.

"Leave him, Jussy sweetheart," Bubbe says gently. "Jakey is a smart boy. He reminds me of your father when he was young. Always asking questions, and never afraid to tackle the hard ones."

She turns to Jake. "Sweetheart, I'm not going to lie to you. I don't *plan* to die, and there is nothing more I would like to do than to dance with you at your bar mitzvah, or even, Please God, your wedding. But I have to be realistic. I'm an old woman, and I feel very tired. Sometimes when I go to sleep I see your Zayde, almost like he's sitting next to me on the bed."

Bubbe sighs. "I miss him so much."

I squeeze her arm tightly, so tightly she says, "Oy, Jussy, not so hard, *mammele.*" Because I want her to stay here with us, with me, no matter how much she misses Zayde.

"So the will business, Jakey," she continues. "That's just business. It's just an old lady putting her affairs in order. It's nothing to worry about."

Jake starts crying anyway, which of course gets me started.

"Oy, *kinderlach*, you're making me start to cry, too," says Bubbe, her eyes shiny with tears. "What will your mother think if she comes in? She'll think we're crazy!"

Bubbe always manages to make us laugh, even when we're crying. We lie there cuddled together, laughing, crying, and most of all loving, all at the same time.

When I get back up to my room, I feel like praying to someone, anyone, everyone, just as long as they'll help Bubbe get better. After she came here from the rehab unit, it seemed like she was making progress, but now it feels like she's getting a little weaker every day. When she started talking about seeing Zayde before, it really scared me. It also made me feel bad—I mean, I know she loved Zayde and she misses him, but what about me?

The problem with praying is I don't know whom I should pray to anymore. I'm so confused about who I am and what religion I'm supposed to be that just the thought of praying makes me feel sick to my stomach. But I just know I have to pray to something or someone, because even though I get the sick feeling at the thought of doing it, I can't help thinking it's the one thing that might help Bubbe.

I know Bubbe thinks we're all praying to the same person or deity, or whatever you want to call it, and that we just call that person by different names. Most of the time I think she's right, but just in case, I decide I'll cover all the bases and pray to Him or Her by every name I can think of. First I say the *Shema;* since Bubbe's Jewish, I figure I'd better do that first. Then I recite all the Hail Mary—or at least as much as I can remember without my cheat sheet. I don't know any special Muslim prayers, but I make a plea to Allah, asking Him for His help. Then I sit cross-legged on my bedroom floor and meditate. For once I'm not conscious of erupting zits or my butt hurting or even a longing for chocolate. The only thought circling my mind over and over and over is *Please,* please *help Bubbe get better.* I don't even realize till I get up and catch a glimpse of myself in the mirror that there are tears streaming down my face. But I feel better. I don't know if any of my prayers will do any good, but I feel better for having said them. Maybe that's what praying is all about. Maybe it's not just asking God to forgive us for bad things or asking Him for good things. Maybe it's just the act of praying and feeling that there's someone up there listening that makes us feel better and less helpless.

A few days later, when Mrs. McArthur, the school secretary, announces, "Would Justine and Jacob Silver please report to the office?" over the PA system during French class, I'm racking my brain to think of what crime I could have committed, and why they're calling Jake, too. I don't think he's *ever* been in trouble in school, the goody-goody brat.

"Vas-y Justine," says Madame Gobleux, the French teacher, "and take your books with you, just in case."

I love the way Madame Gobleux says my name with her French accent. She makes it sound almost pretty.

I gather up my French books and head to the school office. Dr. Feinstein, the school psychologist, is standing next to Mrs. McArthur's desk, wearing bright chunky jewelry and a concerned expression. I panic, thinking Mom has told her all about the Catholic business and that between them they've decided I've got Deep Psychological Problems and need to see a shrink. I start wondering if this kind of stuff goes on your permanent record. My brain swirls with anxiety as I contemplate the bleak future ahead of me. What college is going to take me if I've got Deep Psychological Problems on my permanent record?

"Hello, Justine, my dear," says Dr. Feinstein in a kindly voice as she puts her arm around my shoulders.

This makes me panic even more. Dr. Feinstein has never

put her arm around me before. Maybe it's a ploy to measure me up for a straitjacket. Suddenly I realize why they called Jake as well as me. They're going to commit me to the Funny Farm and they need Jake to testify I'm crazy.

I'm freaking out, wondering if Jake knows that I "borrowed" his S.U.S.A.N. Decoder Ring without asking so I could go to the Sticky Oaty O's Web site and look up the top-secret strategies so he wouldn't be able to beat me, or if he remembers that I kicked him under the table the other night at dinner. I try to think of something I can bribe him with in return for him testifying that I'm not crazy, just confused.

I'm so busy worrying that I haven't listened to Dr. Feinstein, and wonder why she is ushering me into the principal's office. Then I see Mom sitting in a chair next to the desk. Looking at Mom's face, I just know. This isn't about me being crazy because I wanted to be Catholic. This is about Bubbe.

"Jussy . . ." Mom says, standing up and holding out her arms.

"No, Mom . . . no . . ." I say, shaking my head and refusing to go to her. "It's not true. It *can't* be true. She was fine when I kissed her good-bye this morning. She was just tired."

Mom comes over and hugs me as I stand there stiffly, not wanting to believe her, not wanting to contemplate what the rest of my miserable life will be like without Bubbe in it.

"She took a nap after breakfast and never woke up," Mom says, stroking my hair. "Dr. Stanley said that she probably had a massive stroke, and died in her sleep. He said she didn't suffer."

I feel numb, like the whole world has turned to cotton, and everything—including the fact that I am standing in the principal's office with Mom stroking my hair, and that I kind of like the fact she is doing it because she hardly ever does—seems unreal.

Then the door opens, and Dr. Feinstein brings in Jake. She leaves, shutting the door behind her.

"Hey, Mom, what are you doing here, and what's up with Jussy?" he asks.

Mom reaches out one of the arms that she'd had around me to Jake, and he warily comes over for a hug. He glances over his shoulder to make sure none of his friends are watching, because he knows that if he were caught being hugged by his mom in school, it would be the end of his social existence.

"Jakey, it's Bubbe . . ." Mom says. "She passed away this morning in her sleep. It was very peaceful, just the way she would have wanted it."

Like me, Jake seems to have a problem taking this on board.

"What do you mean, passed away?" he says. "Like, in . . . dead?"

Hearing Jake say it out loud, that horrible, horrible D-word, the one that I've avoided saying since Bubbe's stroke in case it came true, is like a needle piercing through the numb, cottony bubble that has surrounded me ever since I walked into the office and saw Mom. It hits me in the stomach, hard, like someone punched me with brass knuckles on, and I feel like I'm going to throw up. A wave of pain washes over me, a pain so intense that it makes how I felt when I found out that Tommy was dating Athena Johnson seem like a mosquito bite in comparison. I start crying, and it feels like I'll never be able to stop.

My tears convince Jake that *passed away* does indeed mean *dead*, and after standing clenching and unclenching his fists for a few moments, his face turning redder and redder with the effort of trying not to cry, he buries his face in Mom's shoulder and starts crying, too.

It takes a few minutes before I feel, through my own hiccuping sobs, that my mother's shoulders are shaking, too. We stand there in the principal's office, the three of us huddled together, crying over our lost Bubbe.

Chapter Nine

Bubbe's funeral is three days later, on Monday afternoon. Even though I feel guilty about the fact that I was trying to be Catholic, and even guiltier because deep down I can't help wondering if the shock from knowing I was willing to give up what her family died for was what finally killed Bubbe, I still wish we were Catholic. At least Catholics take their time about burying people. Mac told me that when her Great-Aunt Eileen died, she didn't get buried for over a week. They had a wake first, where they all hung out and talked about her aunt and ate and drank a lot.

In Jewish tradition, you have to bury the person first. Then the family sits *shivah* for seven days, which means staying at home with all the mirrors in the house covered so you aren't thinking about how you look and superficial stuff like that. People come over to say prayers every morning and evening, and they always bring food. Why they think you will even be hungry when you are that miserable is beyond me.

I'm even less hungry than I was after Mom found the stuff in my closet. I haven't eaten chocolate since Bubbe died. I figure it's a way of doing penance. I'm thinking of making a vow not to eat chocolate for the rest of my life, but I don't know if I have enough willpower to keep it.

Bubbe's funeral is delayed because she died on Friday, and we couldn't make any funeral arrangements on Saturday because it's Sabbath. I'm glad for the reprieve, because I don't want Bubbe to be buried. I hate the thought of her being in a coffin, and put in the ground. It seems so . . . final.

But time always goes quickest when you don't want it to, and now it's Monday morning. Funeral Day. I'm wearing the same long black skirt I used to wear when I was pretending to be Sister Teresa Benedicta. Helena loaned me a black hair scrunchie without my asking. She just came into my room this morning when I was getting dressed, and offered to do my hair. She brushed it for a few minutes without saying anything and even apologized when she accidentally pulled on a knot and I said "Ow." I wonder if she wants something, or if she's just trying to be nice.

A long black limousine pulls up outside our house, and if I weren't so miserable I'd be excited, because I've never ridden in one before.

We pile into the limo and are driven into Manhattan, to the funeral home on the Upper West Side where the service is to take place.

When we walk into the chapel, I see a simple wood coffin,

and my heart sinks through the bottom of my stomach because I realize that Bubbe is in it.

It looks so small, the coffin. I'm sure she was taller than that when she was alive. Do bodies shrink when they die?

Mrs. Schotstein, Bubbe's downstairs neighbor, who found her after the first stroke, is already there. Standing next to her is the Gonzalez family, who moved in across the hall from Bubbe last year. Mrs. Gonzalez is carrying her baby, Pedro, who's really cute and smiley. He doesn't just barf and cry, like most babies. I'm playing peekaboo with him when I feel an arm around my shoulders. It's Shira. Mrs. Weinstein let her and Sammy skip school to come to the funeral.

"Jussy," she says, and it's enough to get me started again. Pedro stares with his dark, velvety eyes and touches my wet cheek curiously.

Shira and I cling to each other. She's crying, too. Over her shoulder I see Pedro grinning his toothless grin at me, waving his chubby little hand frantically and shouting "Buh!" It makes me laugh at the same time I'm crying. For once, I don't feel like I'm crazy for laughing and crying; they both feel like the right thing to do. Still, I can almost hear Bubbe saying, "Oy, Jussy, stop crying, or you'll make me start crying, too."

Grandma Lila and Grandpa Leo are there. It's weird because it seems like Rabbi Polansky, Bubbe's rabbi, who like all traditionally Orthodox men is sporting a black suit and a thick beard, makes them uncomfortable. Whereas Mrs. Gonzalez, who goes to mass every day without fail, doesn't seem fazed. She chats away with the rabbi like he's her best friend. Go figure.

We sit down in the front row and the funeral service begins. The rabbi recites prayers in Hebrew, which we read in English when he is done. Then Dad stands and walks slowly up to the lectern. He places his reading glasses on the end of his nose and pulls a few folded sheets of paper from the inside pocket of his dark suit. He looks grave and sad.

"My mother, Zofia, might have appeared frail, but she possessed a strength of character that allowed her to survive horrors we can't even begin to imagine."

Dad goes on to talk about Bubbe's early life in Szged, Hungary. He tells everyone how she grew up surrounded by a large and loving family, one that she never saw again after they were deported to Auschwitz in May 1944. Bubbe, the oldest of her nine brothers and sisters, survived the selection process because she was young and fit enough to do forced labor.

Dad recounts how she and Zayde Sam met in a displaced-persons camp at the end of the war. Zayde had lost all of his family, too, so they shared that feeling of being all alone in the world.

When Dad says how the loss of Bubbe's entire family during the war made the birth of her three grandchildren even more special than it was for other grandparents, Jake sniffs loudly, and starts fumbling in his pocket for one of the tissues that Mom gave us before the service. Helena is quiet, but out of the corner of my eye I can see her cheeks have brown mascara tracks running down them. The tissue I'm using is starting to disintegrate from overuse, and I still feel like I could cry for a month without stopping.

The rabbi cuts the black ribbons of mourning we're all wearing. They sometimes cut people's clothes, to symbolize how, in the Bible, people "rent their garments" when someone died, but I can't imagine Dad letting anyone near his Hermès tie with a pair of scissors, even if he is in mourning. These days, most people use ribbons instead.

We pile back into the limousine, and a procession of cars with their headlights on follows us to the cemetery. A big hole has been dug next to Zayde's grave, and we gather around as Bubbe's plain wooden coffin is lowered in. The tree next to Zayde's grave is in bloom, and birds are singing nearby. It's not fair that everything is so beautiful and alive. It's too nice a day for someone to be put in the ground forever.

After Dad says Kaddish, the prayer for mourners, he takes a shovel and drops dirt into the grave. It hits the wood of the coffin with a loud thud, and the sound goes right through me because it's so final. I realize this is it—never again will I have someone who loves me the way Bubbe did, with so much love and so little criticism. I have to live the rest of my life without anyone who understands me. It doesn't seem like much to look forward to.

Everyone follows us back to our house, where the mirrors are covered with sheets and the dining-room table groans under the weight of all the food people have brought.

I'm sitting and eating on the sofa in the family room with Jake and Shira (Mom had to relax the rules on eating outside the kitchen for the *shivah*) when Mac and Teresa walk in. I've just taken a huge bite of brownie (so much for my "No Chocolate for Evermore" vow) when I catch a glimpse of Tommy entering the room behind Mac, his tousled blond hair glinting in the light from the chandelier in the hallway. I choke, and brownie crumbs spew out of my mouth in a toxic cloud, spraying Jake, Shira, the sofa, and worst of all, the carpet.

I want to die. Not only have I committed the mortal sin of getting chocolate on the carpet, I've done so in a spectacularly disgusting way in front of Tommy McAllister. Small wonder he prefers Athena Johnson.

Shira and Mac are patting me gently on the back, asking me if I'm okay. Meanwhile, Jake's gaze moves in horrified fascination from the chocolate spew on the carpet to my red, humiliated face.

"That was amazing, Jussy," he says. "Mom is going to kill you."

Thanks, O-he-of-little-comfort. Like I didn't already know.

To make matters worse, Grandma Lila walks in.

"What on earth happened here?" she exclaims. "Look at Adele's new carpet!"

"Yeah, Jussy's dead meat when Mom sees that!" Jake says with gleeful anticipation.

It's hearing the D-word that's the last straw. I leap off the sofa, run upstairs to my room, and slam the door. Throwing myself onto the bed, I burst into hysterical sobs.

I don't know how long I've been crying when the door opens.

"Go away and leave me alone!" I shout angrily.

I don't care who it is. I'm mad at myself for breaking my pledge not to eat chocolate and then being stupid enough to spew brownie all over the living-room carpet just because I saw some guy who doesn't like me anyway. I'm mad at Jake for making me cry in front of Tommy. I'm mad at Tommy for being there when I humiliated myself and for liking Athena Johnson instead of me. I'm mad at Mom for caring more about the carpets than about her children. But most of all—and I feel guilty for even feeling this—I'm mad at Bubbe for dying.

The intruder sits down on the bed next to me and starts stroking my hair.

"Shhh, Jussy darling. Don't worry. It's going to be okay."

It's my mother. She obviously hasn't seen the carpet yet. Although the Wrath of Mom is about the last thing I feel like facing right now, I figure the rest of my life is so devoid of hope that I don't have much to lose by telling her the truth.

"Mom . . ."

"Yes, honey?"

My mother sounds so uncharacteristically gentle that I turn over, sit up, and fling myself into her arms, crying.

"You're going to be m-m-mad at me," I hiccup. "I—I—I sp-spewed brownie on the f-family-room carpet."

"It's okay, sweetheart," Mom says kindly. "I know."

I'm so surprised that she didn't start yelling at me that I stop crying.

"Y-you know?" I sniff incredulously. "And you're not m-mad?"

Mom plucks a tissue from the box on my bedside table and carefully wipes the tears from my cheeks.

"Oh Jussy," she says ruefully. "Am I really that bad?"

She's being so nice to me that I don't want to rock the boat by saying that when it comes to the carpets she really *is* that bad—in fact, probably worse—but my thoughts obviously transmit themselves to my face because Mom bursts out laughing.

"It's all right, sweetheart," she says, giving me a hug. "You don't have to say it. I *have* been a little, well, shall we say, *obsessed* with keeping this house 'just-so.' Maybe I've gone just a teensy bit overboard."

I can't believe 1) that my mom isn't yelling at me, and 2) that she's admitting to this. It just doesn't compute.

Mom kicks off her high heels, lies down on the bed next to me, and brings my head down to rest on her shoulder.

"I know I've always been a bit of a neat freak, but you're right, it's gotten worse. Maybe it's because I've been feeling, well, intimidated since we've moved here," she confesses. "It's so different from New Rochelle. Dad and I went to a dinner party a few months ago, and the whole thing was catered, complete with a butler serving. Can you imagine? Our idea of a dinner party has always been sitting around the kitchen table with the Weinsteins."

Mom sighs heavily. "I guess deep down I don't feel 'grown up' enough to be going to dinner parties with butlers."

I'm dumbstruck. I never would have imagined, not in a million years, that my beautiful, slim, elegantly dressed mother could be intimidated by anything.

"Do you miss living in New Rochelle?" I ask her tentatively. We've never really talked about the move.

"I suppose I do," Mom admits. "I miss having the Weinsteins around the corner, and having neighbors close enough to say hello."

"But haven't you made new friends here?" I ask. She and Dad always seem to be going out to something or other—when they're not fighting about Armando and Marcel, that is.

"Of course we have. But Annette Weinstein and I have been friends for, well, since we met in Lamaze class when we were pregnant with you and Shira. And how old are you now?"

The warm fuzzy feeling I've been experiencing evaporates. I can't believe my *own mother* can't remember how old I am. I mean she was *there,* wasn't she?

"I bet you remember how old Helena is!" I mutter angrily.

Mom turns to me and opens her mouth to speak. But I'm on a roll. All the angry hurt I've been feeling about Bubbe dying, about Tommy liking Athena Johnson, about the fact that life is so unjust and I'm the least loved of my parents' offspring, wells up and bursts out of me in an explosion of nuclear proportion.

"You would never forget anything about *Saint Helena,*" I shout bitterly. "She's always been your favorite. And all Dad ever wanted was a boy. It's obvious Jake's *his* favorite. I bet you guys wish you never had me. You even love that stupid poodle more than you love me!"

I stop and suddenly realize that I've said all the things that I've felt forever but never thought I'd say. Part of me wishes I could take it back, because now I'm afraid. Afraid I've let the demon out of the black hole inside me, and scared of what might happen as a result.

Mom is staring at me, astonished. Then she cups my cheek in her hand. I'm amazed to see that her eyes are glistening with tears.

"Oh Jussy, darling," she says in a quavery voice. "I had no idea . . . of course I don't love Helena more than you. You children are the best thing I've ever done with my life—each of you in your own special way."

Despite the fact that Mom seems genuine, I'm not convinced. It sounds like the sort of thing that parents know they're supposed to say to their kids, whether they really feel that way or not. I mean what parent in their right mind is going to come out and say, "Well, actually, honey, you're right. I do love your older sister more"?

Mom sits up, reaches for a tissue, and blots the mascara from under her eyes.

"I suppose I understand Helena better, because she's more like me in a lot of ways," she says. "But that doesn't mean I love her more."

Mom looks at me, almost shyly. "In fact, while we're doing 'True Confessions,' *I've* always thought you loved Bubbe more than you loved me. Ever since you were tiny, the two of you have been exceptionally close. I suppose I always felt a bit left out."

Now it's my turn to be astonished.

"You were jealous of Bubbe?" I ask incredulously.

Mom nods. "Yes, in a way I was. She always seemed to be able to get things right with you, whereas I . . ." She looks at me sadly. "I always seem to get it wrong."

"Not always," I say, trying to reassure her. Then I realize how it must have sounded. "I mean . . . well . . ."

I trail off, not sure how to dig my ever-present foot out of my mouth. I feel the familiar rush of anger with myself for blowing it when, for once, I was on my mom's good side. But Mom just starts laughing. And finally, so do I. We lie side by side on my bed, laughing and crying at the same time.

Chapter Ten

It's really hard to go back to school the following week. Everyone else's life has gone on as usual; school, homework, music, boys. But for me it feels like normal life ended when Bubbe died. Even though things are better with Mom since the night of the funeral, I feel lost and lonely without Bubbe around.

It's even worse because I know that if it weren't for me, she would still be here. Guilt presses down on me like a two-hundred-ton weight. Sometimes, for a few blissful moments, I forget that Bubbe's dead, and I head toward the guest room to tell her something. But then it'll hit me. A heavy fog descends, and I wonder if I'll ever feel normal again, not that I felt that normal to begin with. But even the miserable, confused eleven-almost-twelve-year-old I was before beats how I feel now.

The other night I got back into my closet with Father Ted and confessed about how I killed Bubbe. I thought it would make me feel better, but it didn't. I don't know if it's because I don't have the cross and the rosary beads anymore, or because I couldn't remember the words of the Hail Mary without my cheat sheet. But I felt just as bad when I left the closet as I did before I went in.

So I've decided more drastic measures are called for. I tell Mom that I have to meet Mac at the library on Saturday afternoon at three, but after she drops me off, I head toward the nearest Catholic church, St. Clare's. Even though St. Bernadette's, Mac's church, is also nearby, the memories of the disastrous mass I went to with the McAllisters are still fresh. I can't imagine showing my face at St. Bernadette's ever again, except maybe to be a bridesmaid in Mac's wedding, "God willing, someday," as Bubbe always said.

I'm nervous as I sneak up the front steps of St. Clare's and glance around to make sure I don't see any of my parents' friends; or, more to the point, that *they* don't see *me.*

I'm feeling guilty, for a change. I feel guilty that I'm going into a Catholic church, especially on a Saturday. Deep down I wonder if I should be going to synagogue instead. But I'm supposed to be Catholic now, so go figure.

Taking a deep breath, I open the heavy oak door. It's dim inside the church after the glare of the sunny afternoon outside. The spicy-sweet smell of incense tickles my nose. It's unfamiliar, but strangely comforting.

The church is empty. It says on the sign outside that confession starts at three-thirty, but I wanted to get here early. I figure if I scope out the lay of the land, maybe I won't make a fool out of myself when it comes time for confession.

I look around for some clue about where people go to confess. There are some wooden doors that look like closets on the right-hand side of the church, and I figure they must be the confessionals. I head toward the doors, past a statue of the Virgin Mary holding Baby Jesus.

I stop and stare at a big painting of Jesus on the cross, fascinated by how lifelike and sad Jesus' eyes look, but weirded out at the same time by how it shows Jesus' wounds in such gory detail.

Being here makes me feel strange. It's like there are two people inside me, one telling me that I'm doing the right thing and another that's saying that I'm betraying my family and my people and everything they believed in and died for over the centuries.

"Have you come for confession?"

Startled, I turn around and see this really cute guy. He's young, with brown eyes, and dark curly hair. He's wearing black, with a white collar around his neck. Oh no. *Please* don't tell me he's the priest.

"Uh . . . yeah," I manage to stammer.

"I'm Father Joseph," he says. "But most people call me Father Joe. Monsignor Camas is away today, so I'm taking confession."

I was expecting someone old and wrinkled, with gray hair, not this guy who looks like a movie star in a priest costume.

Just as I'm about to turn tail and run out of the church as fast as my legs will carry me, the cute priest says, "It's a little early, but since you're here we might as well get started. Do you want to confess face-to-face or in the confessional?"

I have no idea what I'm supposed to do. In the movies people go into a booth and a little trapdoor opens in the wall to reveal the priest behind a mesh screen. All you ever see is the vague shadow of a face and a talking mouth.

"Uh . . . the confessional," I manage to stutter. "If that's okay with you."

"However you feel more comfortable," he says kindly.

There's no way I'd feel more comfortable sitting face-to-face with Father Joseph, because I know I'd end up committing the Deadly Sin of lust right when I'm supposed to be confessing and clearing my conscience.

How do people ever manage to end up with a clean slate? My sins mount up so quickly I'd have to spend my whole life in confession to have a clean slate. And if Father Joseph is the person I'm confessing to, I'll never get there. I wonder—do you get double time in purgatory for having a crush on a priest?

Father Joe opens one of the doors and gestures for me to go into the one next to it. I enter what feels like a dark wooden closet. There's nowhere to sit, just a little cushion on the floor in front of the mesh screen, so I guess I'm supposed to kneel.

I think about all the sins that must have been revealed in this tiny claustrophobic space over the years. If only the walls could talk. Then I wonder if sins are catching, you know, like whatever it is your mother warns you you might catch if you sit on a public toilet seat. Maybe I am my mother's daughter after all, thinking about that kind of stuff. Out of all the things I could have inherited from her, why did I end up getting her obsessive-compulsive genes? That's what I'd like to know.

A trapdoor opens on the other side of the mesh screen, and I see the shadowy outline of Father Joseph's chin on the other side of the screen. At least *something* is like it is in the movies. But I wish I hadn't seen Father Joseph before the confession, 'cause now I find myself distracted by the thought of his brown eyes and curly dark hair. *Concentrate, Justine, concentrate!*

"Forgive me, Father, for I have sinned," I start in a quavery voice. "It's been . . ."

I hesitate, trying to remember when I last confessed to Father Ted. Does confessing to a teddy bear count?

"Uh . . . about four days since my last confession."

There's silence on the other side of the screen. I panic, wondering if I've got it wrong and Father Joseph's whipped out his cell phone to call the Vatican and report me to the pope.

After what's probably a minute but feels like an hour, Father Joseph says gently, "Is there something you'd like to tell me?"

"Oh! Uh . . . yeah," I say. I don't want to launch right into my major sins, so I figure I'll start off with a few minor ones. I'm new at the business of confessing to a real priest, and I need to get warmed up.

"I stole my brother Jake's S.U.S.A.N. Decoder Ring without him knowing so that I could look up the secret strategies on the Sticky Oaty O's Web site and beat him," I tell Father Joseph.

"I see," Father Joe says, with something that sounds suspiciously like amusement in his voice.

I wonder if it's because he thinks my sin is juvenile, so I figure I better move to the Deadly Ones.

"I have the Deadly Sin of envy," I tell him, anxious to prove that I'm a serious sinner, not a childish one. "I envy Mac because she has a dream mom who is understanding and makes cookies instead of buying them. I envy Athena Johnson because she's got long tan legs and is a cheerleader, and because Tommy likes her instead of me."

Worried that I'm about to forget something, I reach into

my pocket and take out Father Ted's checklist of Deadly Sins. It's hard to read in the dim light of the confessional.

"Oh, yeah, then there's gluttony and greed. I've combined them because they both have to do with chocolate. I made a vow not to eat chocolate after my Bubbe, uh, I mean my grandmother . . . died, but . . ."

My eyes start to prickle when I think of Bubbe.

"I guess it's that gluttony thing. I can't seem to get through the day at the moment without eating at least one big chocolate bar. Sometimes it takes two or three."

I stop for a moment in case Father Joseph wants a chance to say something, but the outline of his chin is still and silent, so I carry on.

"Then there's sloth. According to my mom, I'm incredibly slothful, although she doesn't use that word exactly. She's always complaining about the state of my bedroom."

The next sin on the list is pride, but I don't have anything to feel proud about, so I figure I can skip that one. After pride comes lust. There's no way on earth, not for any amount of money or even the fear of hellfire, that I'm going to talk to Father Joseph about lust, even if it is only his mouth and chin I'm speaking to. So I move on to the last one, anger.

"This will prove to you what an awful person I am. I'm angry at my Bub—I mean my grandmother because she died and left me. But what's even worse is that . . ."

I start to cry.

"What's even worse is that I killed her!" I sob.

As usual, there are no tissues in my pocket when I need them. I end up blowing my nose on the list of Seven Deadly Sins. It sounds extra loud in the confines of the confessional. Father Joe must think I'm disgusting, as well as being a sinner.

"It's quite common for bereaved people to feel anger toward the loved ones who have left them behind," says Father Joe gently. "I wouldn't consider that to be a Deadly Sin. But . . . could you explain to me how exactly you killed your Bubbe?"

I'm so upset that the fact that he's said Bubbe instead of Grandmother doesn't sink in. In between hiccups, I wonder how I can explain what I did without having to tell Father Joseph that I'm not really Catholic, I'm an impostor. Try as I might, I can't think of any way to do it. I decide to tell Father Joe the truth, and throw myself on his mercy.

"It was the shock," I tell him. "You see, Father Joseph, I'm . . . I'm . . . I'mnotreallyCatholic."

There's silence from the other side of the screen, and I wonder if Father Joe is back on his cell phone, this time calling the Heavenly Hosts to come zap me with a thunderbolt or two.

"No," he says quietly. "I didn't think you were."

"You didn't." I sniffle, amazed. "What gave me away?"

Father Joseph laughs. "I wondered because you looked so

nervous out there," he says. "Like you'd never done this before. And then when you said, 'Bubbe' . . ."

"I knew that would give me away," I mutter, angry at myself for the slip.

"It might not have with Monsignor Camas," Father Joe says. "But you can probably tell by the way I talk that I grew up on Long Island.

"I'm from Massapequa," he continues. "It's a town with a big population of Jews and Italian Catholics. People call it 'MatzoPizza.' You can probably figure out which category I fall under."

Despite my tears, I giggle.

"A lot of my good friends were Jewish, and some of them had Bubbes and Zaydes," continues Father Joe. "I learned bits of Yiddish from them."

Who would have imagined? A Yiddish-speaking Catholic priest. God really *does* move in mysterious ways.

"So I'm intrigued. How exactly did you kill your Bubbe?" asks Father Joe. "Would you be willing to talk to me about it?"

I begin to tell him, and the tears start flowing again. Having saturated Father Ted's Seven Deadly Sins list with the first deluge, I end up having to wipe my eyes with the bottom of my shirt. I tell Father Joe everything, from how I'd wanted to start keeping kosher to my confessions in the closet with Father Ted. I tell him about going to mass with the McAllisters and how God took it out on Bubbe instead of punishing me. Finally, I tell him about the mouse and the Not-Anywhere Anytime Pest service, and how Mom found the stuff in my closet.

"So it was the shock that killed her." I sniffle. "Here she was, tortured during the war for being Jewish, and her granddaughter was going to give it all up."

Father Joseph is silent when I finish, and I imagine it's because he's thinking how awful I am, for being sacrilegious with the rosary and Mac's cross, and for killing my own grandmother. But he surprises me.

"You know, we really have to work on your image of God," he says kindly. "I don't picture God as 'the Great Enforcer,' whose goal is to punish us every time we make a mistake. I think of God waiting for us with open arms, hoping that we seek Him out. Your Bubbe's death wasn't your fault. It was nature taking its course in an elderly lady who had been through a lot."

Father Joe is silent for a moment.

"Now, as for you becoming Catholic, I'd advise you to take your time," he says. "I don't think anyone should make major life decisions when they are bereaved if they can possibly help it. By the way, how old are you?"

"Eleven," I tell him. "But I'm almost twelve."

"So you have time to decide," Father Joseph says. "If you decide you truly want to convert to Catholicism, then you'll have plenty of time to learn what you need to know before confirmation. And in the meantime . . ."

He pauses for a moment.

"In the meantime what?" I ask.

"In the meantime, I would suggest that you talk to your rabbi. And no matter which road you decide to take on your life's journey, just make sure God is an intimate part of it," Father Joe tells me. "You are a girl who has faith, which is a rare thing in today's world.

"And may God bless you as you struggle with your decision," he adds.

I feel a warm glow inside, because Father Joe sees me as a Girl Who Has Faith, instead of a snot-nosed, sniveling sinner.

"Shouldn't I say some Hail Marys or something?" I ask him. "You know, for penance."

I'm kind of hoping he says no, because I can't remember all the words.

"I don't think that's necessary," Father Joe says, and through the screen it sounds like he is smiling. "Go with God, young lady. You're a very special girl."

I can feel myself starting to blush up a storm, and I'm glad that Father Joe's on the other side of the screen so he can't see me.

"Thank you, Father. Thanks. Uh . . . Bye," I stammer, and

quickly push the door open to leave so I don't make even more of a fool of myself.

Even the dim light of the church seems bright after the darkness of the confessional. There's a line of people waiting to confess. I keep my head down as I walk by because I don't want them to see my red eyes and tearstained face.

Back at the library I head straight to the bathroom to wash my face and put on some of the mango-flavored glitter lip gloss I stole from Helena's makeup collection. I still look pretty awful, but at least I have glittery lips.

I've got an hour left until Mom picks me up. I decide to go look up some books about Judaism. I have to try to figure out what being Jewish is all about. Grandma Lila and Grandpa Leo see it one way. They don't keep kosher because they think the dietary laws are antiquated, and they hardly ever go to synagogue. They give lots of money to Jewish causes and belong to a Jewish country club. I get the impression that for them, being Jewish is more about community than spirituality.

For Bubbe it was different. She kept kosher and went to synagogue every Shabbat, but being Jewish for Bubbe wasn't just about observing rituals. She seemed to really believe in God. It used to surprise me that she believed in Him despite the fact He'd let the Nazis kill off all her family. I even asked her about it once.

"So many tragic things happen, *mammele,* that seem unfathomable and unfair," Bubbe said. "We get angry at God, because we aren't able to see the entire tapestry of the divine plan. I could have lost faith after Auschwitz. A lot of people who survived did. But for me, it was faith that kept me going when I wanted to give up. I knew that God meant for me to fulfill a purpose in life, that didn't include dying at the hands of the Nazi beasts."

I wonder if God's divine plan for me includes being Catholic. I've tried asking Him about it when I pray, but He hasn't been very forthcoming.

Then there's my parents. They're like a mixture of both sets of grandparents, which, I suppose, is hardly surprising. Mom prepares the chicken meal every Friday night and lights candles, and my parents send us to Hebrew school, but they hardly ever go to synagogue themselves. It's like they've reduced being Jewish to chicken soup and chopped liver. There's got to be more to it than that.

I decide I need to do some research. My parents and grandparents have confused the issue so much, I guess this is something that I'm going to have to figure out for myself.

Chapter Eleven

At breakfast on Thursday morning, Dad tells us Mr. Rothstein is coming over that evening to read Bubbe's will. I'm more excited by Mom's announcement that the Weinsteins are coming for brunch a week from Sunday. They're going to bring bagels and lox from the deli in New Rochelle and Shira's cousins Robert and Amie, who are visiting that weekend.

Mr. Rothstein arrives at eight o'clock. Mom and Dad take him into the fancy living room. Jake and I are playing S.U.S.A.N. in the family room, and thanks to the secret tips I learned from the Sticky Oaty O's Web site when I "borrowed" Jake's decoder ring, I'm very close to finding the Top Secret Formula. He can't understand why he's not beating me. Well, they say all's fair in love and war.

At about quarter to nine Mom tells us to come into the living room.

"Where's Helena?" she asks.

Stupid question. Jake and I reply, almost in unison, "On the phone."

"Well, go tell her she should hang up and come down straightaway," Mom says firmly. "Mr. Rothstein has something to say to you."

Neither Jake nor I relish the idea of having to try to detach Helena from the telephone. She's either talking to the boy du jour or gossiping to her girlfriends about him. Jake's the youngest, so I make him go. There have got to be *some* perks to make up for being the Tormented Middle Child.

Jake bounds up the stairs shouting, "*Helena!* Mom says to hang up the phone and get your butt down to the living room this instant!"

Mom and I hear Helena's distant shriek in response, and Mom sighs heavily as she puts her arm around my shoulders and guides me into the living room.

"I'm sure I didn't say it in *exactly* those words," she says.

"No, not *exactly*," I agree, and I'm happy to see I've made her smile.

Mr. Rothstein stands politely when I enter the living room with Mom.

"And you must be . . . ?" he asks.

"Justine," I say, shaking his hand. I'm still basking in the glow from Mom's approval, and want to show Mr. Rothstein that at least *one* of her children has manners.

"Ah, Justine," says Mr. Rothstein, examining me thoughtfully as we sit down. "Your grandmother always spoke especially highly of you."

I get a warm feeling inside from his words, but it's followed by the sinking realization that Bubbe's no longer here to speak especially highly of me. She's no longer here, period.

Mom, who's sitting next to me on the couch, senses my change of mood and reaches for my hand. It's funny. Ever since we had that talk in my bedroom the day of Bubbe's funeral, it's like Mom understands me better. Or maybe I just understand her better. Maybe it's a little of both.

Mr. Rothstein reaches into his briefcase and hands me an envelope and a small leather jewelry box.

"Your grandmother wanted you to have this," he said.

I turn over the envelope and see my name written in Bubbe's spiky, old-fashioned handwriting. My eyes prickle.

Mom squeezes my hand. "You don't have to read it now, not if you don't feel up to it," she says gently. "You can wait until you're ready."

"It's okay." I sniff, wishing that I had a tissue, and I smile gratefully at Mom when she hands me one.

With trembling fingers, I open the envelope, careful not to rip it. I want to save it because my name's on it in Bubbe's handwriting. I think of all the birthday-card envelopes I threw away carelessly because I knew another one would come the following year. I wish I could get them all back.

It's hard to read the letter, because the handwriting is really shaky. I see it's dated a few days before Bubbe died, so it must have been a big effort for her to write.

My darling Justine,

I know you are going through a lot of confusion right now, about who you are and what you believe. Don't worry so much, mammele. *It's normal. Young people have always questioned what their parents tell them. It's how they learn to be good grown-ups.*

I want you to have this necklace. It's one that your Zayde Sam had made for me, but I never wore. I think it's because after being forced to wear a star by the Nazis, I never wanted to wear one again. Zayde knew I felt this way, and that's the reason he got me the necklace. He told me, "Zofia, I'm going to make you a star so beautiful that you will wear it with pride, the way the Star of David should be worn." But even though it was beautiful, I couldn't bring myself to wear it. I see now that it was a mistake, and I know it made your Zayde sad, but he still loved me, even if he didn't understand.

That's how I feel about you wanting to be Catholic, my darling Justine. It's hard for me to comprehend, but I will always love you, even if I don't understand. Just do your old

Bubbe a favor and "check out" your Jewish heritage before you make a final decision. That way if you still think you should be Catholic, you'll know that you're doing it because it means something to you, not just because you are ashamed of who you are. Although what a beautiful, smart girl like you has to be ashamed of I don't know. If you aren't proud of who and what you are, then changing the name of the person you pray to won't make you feel any better. You know, Jussy, I've always thought all these different names mean the same G-d anyway. It's just the rituals that separate us. If everyone felt the same way, this world we live in would be a much more peaceful place.

I trust you to make a good decision, and I trust G-d to help you get there.

So, Jussy darling, I hope someday you will wear this necklace and that it will give you as much pleasure as knowing you has given me. When you put it on, you'll know that Zayde and I are up in heaven, smiling. Remember, even if we aren't physically present, we'll always be there watching over you and surrounding you with our love. No one could have asked for a more wonderful granddaughter.

Your loving Bubbe

I'm a total mess by the time I finish. Mom, who has been reading the letter over my shoulder, is crying, too. I can't believe that Bubbe trusted me to make the right decision, when it's patently obvious that I'm as confused as a girl can be. I can't figure out if it's because she loved me, trusted in God, or both.

I pick up the jewelry box and open it. Inside is a diamond Star of David, on a delicate, silvery chain. The diamonds glint and sparkle in the light from the chandelier.

"It's so . . . beautiful," I exclaim tearfully.

Dad, who has been sitting quietly by the fireplace in one of the overstuffed armchairs holding his head in his hands, looks up.

"Come here, Jussy sweetheart," he says quietly. "Show me the necklace."

I cross the room and sit on my father's lap, holding out the jewelry box for him so he can see Bubbe's gift. He looks at it without saying anything, then lifts it gently out of the box.

"Here, let me put it on for you," he says. "Do you want me to put it on?"

I nod, because I don't trust my voice.

Dad puts the necklace around my neck and does up the clasp. Then he looks up at me, and I notice that his eyes are red and full of tears.

"I never saw my mother wear this necklace," he says. "She must have been saving it for you all these . . ."

He chokes on a sob. I throw my arms around his neck and our tears mingle on his cheek.

Jake and Helena come in, bickering, but they stop abruptly when they see us crying.

"What's up with Jussy and Dad?" Jake says worriedly.

"Jacob, Helena, where are your manners?" Mom says. "Please say hello to Bubbe's lawyer, Mr. Rothstein."

Jake shuffles over and shakes hands with Mr. Rothstein, still eyeing Dad and me anxiously.

"So you must be Jacob," Mr. Rothstein says jovially. He reaches into his briefcase and pulls out a velvet pouch. "Your grandmother left this for you."

Reaching into his briefcase again, he brings out a small jewelry box and hands it to Helena. "And this, my dear, is for you."

Jake pulls a gold pocket watch on a thick chain out of the velvet pouch.

"That was your great-grandfather's," Dad says. "Zayde's father, who died in the Holocaust. He hid it with a few pieces of my grandmother's jewelry behind a fireplace brick. Zayde went back after the war and found it. Bring it here, Jakey."

Jake carries the watch as if it's made of breakable china, and hands it to Dad. Dad presses down the crown, and the watch begins to chime.

"Cool!" Jake exclaims in wonderment. "Let me try!"

Meanwhile, Helena has opened her box to find Bubbe's pearl necklace with the ruby clasp, the one she wore every Shabbat.

We sit in the living room wearing Bubbe's jewelry, wishing that she were here to see us. I try to imagine Bubbe and Zayde up in heaven, looking down at us and smiling.

Chapter Twelve

I still don't understand why Bubbe had such trust in my decision-making abilities given my disastrous record to date. But her letter gives me confidence to continue my quest to find out what Judaism is all about—at least for me.

Ever since my visit to the library after seeing Father Joe, I've been reading books on the topic. I keep them hidden in my bedside table, and when I hear Mom coming in to say good night, I hide whichever book I'm reading under the covers and pretend to read Harry Potter for the zillionth time.

"You're reading Harry Potter *again*?" Mom asks incredulously. "This town has one of the best libraries in the country, and you can't find something else to read?"

"I just felt like it," I tell her, although even to me my protest rings hollow.

I can't understand why I feel compelled to hide the fact that I'm reading about Judaism from my mom. After all the fuss she made about me wanting to be Catholic, you'd think she'd be over the moon that I want to learn more about my own faith. But sometimes I get the feeling that Mom wants me to be Jewish without being too Jewish, if you know what I mean. It's confusing when your family is mad at you for not wanting to be something and then upset if you want to be it too much.

Mom kisses me good night and leaves the room with Bijoux trailing at her heels. As soon as she's out of sight, I take *The Complete Idiot's Guide to Understanding Judaism* from its hiding place under the covers. It's amazing how little I know, despite suffering through years of Hebrew school. I mean, I can tell you about all the rituals we do and why we celebrate all the holidays. I can read the prayers in Hebrew, but if the English translations weren't on the opposite page, I wouldn't have a clue what they mean. But I still don't understand what's at the core of our faith.

Maybe it's time to take Father Joseph's advice and go talk to a rabbi. For some reason I don't feel right about speaking to Rabbi Bernheim at the synagogue my parents belong to. I'm not sure why. Maybe because I'm afraid he'll talk to my parents, and I feel too vulnerable to share this with my family. I can't face the teasing. I can just hear Helena saying: "Here goes Jussy with another of her phases."

I wonder if there's Rabbi/Justine privilege like there is between lawyers and criminals. I'm pretty sure priests aren't allowed to tell what people say in the confessional. Can rabbis?

I'm about to go look it up on the Internet when I remember about the new place in town. I'm not sure exactly what it is, because it's called the Center for Jewish Understanding instead of Temple or Synagogue. Hannah, a girl in my Hebrew-school class, told me she went to a Purim party there. Most importantly, it's not a place I'd expect to see any of my parents' friends, so I decide to give it a try.

On Saturday morning I put on my Sister Teresa Benedicta skirt and ask Mom if she can drop me off at Starbucks so I can meet Mac to go shopping. I feel bad about lying, but somehow I don't think Mom will understand. I'll just add it to the fast-growing list of sins I have to confess on Yom Kippur. I hope I don't run out of paper before then.

"That's fine," Mom says. "I'm dropping Helena off at the top of the avenue. She wants to buy something new to wear for her date tonight. Apparently she has a new boyfriend."

I roll my eyes. Parents can be *so* clueless.

"Helena's *always* going out with someone new," I tell Mom. "If she buys a different outfit every time she goes out with a new boy, her wardrobe is going to take over the house."

Mom laughs. Then she notices that I'm wearing Bubbe's Star of David.

"Honey, I really don't think you should wear Bubbe's

necklace to go shopping," she says. "What if you lose it? You'll feel terrible. It's not even insured yet."

Nice work, Justine, I tell myself. *Why didn't you have the brains to put it inside your T-shirt?*

Then I start to thinking about what would happen if I *did* lose Bubbe's necklace. I don't think having it insured would help, because even if the insurance company bought me another one that looked exactly the same, I'd know it wasn't the one Bubbe gave me. Still, the insurance angle gives me an idea.

"I thought I'd stop in at Rossmann's Jewelers and get them to appraise it for the insurance," I tell Mom.

She smiles. "Good thinking, sweetheart. But maybe you should tuck it inside your shirt. Greenwich is a safe place, but I still don't think you should walk around town with a diamond Star of David flashing on your chest."

I can't help wondering if she says this because she's really worried about someone robbing me, or if she thinks my necklace is just a diamond equivalent of the yellow star Bubbe had to wear during the war.

Mom drops Helena at the top of Greenwich Avenue and then leaves me at Starbucks. When I'm sure her car is out of sight, I walk a few blocks to the Jewish Understanding place. I hesitate a few minutes on the doorstep. What if they all look at me funny because I'm not a member? What happens if I do something stupid? Will I be kicked out and told never to come back?

I take Bubbe's necklace out from under my shirt and grip the star in my palm.

"Bubbe," I whisper. "Can you ask God to help me figure out how to do the right thing? You're in His neighborhood now, so it's local instead of long distance. Put in a good word for me, okay? Thanks, Bubbe."

I take a deep breath, open the door, and walk in. The service has already started. The place is small, but cozy, kind of like being in someone's living room.

I take a seat at the back, trying to be inconspicuous. The rabbi is reading from the Torah, and a little boy is standing on a chair looking over the rabbi's shoulder as he reads. A bunch of little kids are walking around sucking noisily on lollipops, but no one's giving them dirty looks or telling them "shush."

It's noisy and chaotic, but I don't feel weird and out of place, the way I did when I went to church with the McAllisters. I close my eyes, listening to the rabbi half sing, half chant the Torah portion. The sound of Hebrew is familiar and . . . comforting. Suddenly I feel that Bubbe is very close, and I'm afraid to move in case she goes away.

"Would you like a prayer book?"

Startled, I open my eyes. A pretty woman carrying a little

girl with curly hair is offering me a book so I can follow along with the Torah portion.

"Thanks," I say gratefully.

The little girl waves at me, and I wave back.

"She's so cute," I say to the woman.

"This is my daughter, Rivka," she says. "I'm Miriam Freeman. My husband is the rabbi. We haven't met yet, have we?"

"I don't think so. I've never been here before," I tell her. "I'm Justine. Justine Silver."

"Welcome, Justine," she says. "I'm so glad you could come."

She sits next to me and points out where the rabbi is in the reading from the Torah portion.

"Do you live in Greenwich?" she whispers.

"Uh, yeah. But I don't belong here," I whisper back sheepishly. "My family belongs to the Conservative synagogue. I just came because I wanted to ask the rabbi some questions. I hope that's okay."

"Everybody 'belongs' here," she says with a smile. "No membership required. And there's nothing my husband loves more than a young person asking questions. Stay for kiddush after the service, then you can ask him all the questions you want. I'll make sure to introduce you."

A woman comes in, and Mrs. Freeman gets up to greet her. I start to read the Torah portion in English. The passage is about this guy Korach, who leads a rebellion against Moses when the Children of Israel are wandering around in the desert after they leave Egypt. God gets mad, so He makes the earth crack open and swallow the rebels up.

I get a sick feeling in the pit of my stomach as I read. If God gets this upset by Korach rebelling against Moses, how is He going to feel about me going to confession with Father Joseph? I glance nervously at the floor by my feet, checking for cracks, but I can't see if there are any because of the wall-to-wall carpeting. I know Father Joe said that God isn't "the Great Enforcer," but I offer up a quick but fervent apology just in case.

After the service, we head to another room for kiddush. It's quite a spread. The rabbi says the blessings over the wine and the challah. After everyone's had a sip of wine and a piece of challah, people start helping themselves to food.

I'm standing to one side, shy and embarrassed. I mean, it's not like I've paid dues or anything, so I feel bad helping myself to their Sabbath meal. But a dapper elderly man in a blue suit and a bright red bow tie comes over and hands me a plate.

"*Ess! Ess!* As my mother used to say." He grins. He speaks with a heavy accent, like Bubbe. "You look hungry."

"Um . . . Can I ask you a question?" I whisper.

He tilts his balding head toward me and whispers, "A question? Sure! Ask as many as you like. I answer questions free of charge on Shabbos." He winks at me and adds, "Especially for pretty girls."

I blush, because he thinks I'm pretty. He might be old enough to be my grandfather, but I'll take compliments wherever I can get them.

"Is it okay to eat if I'm not a member?" I ask him.

"Everyone and no one is a member here," he says. "We're always happy to welcome a new face. Especially one as cute as yours," he adds, his blue eyes twinkling.

An elegant, snowy-haired lady comes up behind him and puts her hands on his slightly stooped shoulders.

"Are you flirting with the pretty girls again?" she says indignantly, but I can tell she's not really upset. I still can't get over the fact that two people have said I'm pretty in five minutes. I could get used to this.

The lady puts out a slim, wrinkled hand adorned by the biggest emerald-and-diamond ring I've ever seen.

"I'm Selma Maisner," she says. "This old reprobate is my husband, Murray."

"I'm Justine," I tell her as I shake her hand. "Justine Silver."

"Nice to meet you, Justine," says Mrs. Maisner. "Help yourself to the buffet before Murray gets there or you won't get any lox."

I help myself to a plate of food, and before I have a chance to wonder where to sit, Mrs. Freeman comes over. True to her word, she introduces me to her husband, the rabbi.

"Aaron, this is Justine Silver," she says. "She's got some questions for you."

I was hoping she'd forgotten about the question part. If I manage to eat, drink, and ask questions all at the same time without spilling anything on the rabbi, it'll be a sure sign that 1) there is a God, and 2) He wants me to be Jewish.

I sit across the table from the rabbi, who has a little boy on his lap.

"Good Shabbos, Justine," the rabbi says. "Welcome."

"Thanks," I reply. I'm not really sure how to start, so I spread some chopped liver on the challah and take a bite or two. The rabbi is feeding his son *cholent,* a Sabbath stew made with meat, potatoes, and beans. I don't know why, but watching the rabbi feed his son makes him less formidable. I'm suddenly not as scared to ask him questions because he seems human instead of rabbi-like.

"Rabbi, I'm very confused and I need to learn what Judaism is all about," I blurt out in a rush. So much for leading up to it slowly.

"You need to learn what Judaism is all about," the rabbi repeats thoughtfully. "Hmm . . ."

He picks up a cup and carefully helps the little boy drink

some grape juice. The boy ends up with a grape-juice mustache, curling in a purple semicircle from his upper lip.

"There's a story from the Talmud that might help," Rabbi Freeman says. "It tells of an idol worshiper who came to one of the Sages, Rabbi Shammai, and said, 'If you can teach me the whole Torah while I stand on one foot, you can convert me to Judaism.' Rabbi Shammai was angered by the man's disrespect and sent him away."

He spoons some more *cholent* into his son's mouth. "So the man went to see another great sage, Rabbi Hillel, and repeated the challenge. Hillel replied, 'What is hateful to you, do not do to your neighbor: that is the whole Torah. The rest is commentary: now go, study.'"

He smiles at me.

"So now you know what Judaism is all about. Are you still confused?" he asks, his eyes twinkling.

"Yeah," I say ruefully. "I'm afraid I am. I guess I need to do the 'go, study' part."

The rabbi lifts his squirming son off his lap, and the little boy makes a beeline for the cookie plate on the buffet. He grabs a brownie and toddles off to join the other kids. It's good to know that even the rabbi's son has a thing for chocolate.

"The 'go study' part is ongoing," the rabbi says, leaning back in his chair. "It's a life's work."

He leans forward, putting his elbows on the table and smiles.

"But every journey has to start somewhere," he says. "And here is as good a place as any. I'm open for questions."

I'm not sure where to start, so I launch in at the middle. I tell him about Grandma and Grandpa, Bubbe, Mom and Dad, and how they all seem to have different views about what Judaism is all about.

The rabbi listens patiently. It feels like he's really taking me seriously. Between him and Father Joseph, this makes two grown-ups who have taken me seriously when I try to talk about religion. It's a whole new experience. Until now, with the exception of Bubbe, no one has *ever* taken me seriously. And even though Bubbe listened, I never felt I could talk to her about Jewish stuff because of what she'd been through during the war.

But I feel comfortable talking to Rabbi Freeman, and I'm on a roll. I end up telling him about being a closet Catholic, and even about my visit to the confessional.

"I'm sorry, Rabbi," I say nervously. "I'm probably going to end up swallowed up by the earth like Korach, aren't I?"

Rabbi Freeman laughs. "I don't think you should lose any sleep over *that* possibility," he says. "And there's no need to apologize to me, Justine. I'm not God's policeman."

He chuckles. "If anything, I'm His salesman. To put it in marketing terms, my job is to educate people about the features and benefits of the Torah lifestyle."

"So what do I do?" I ask him. "How do I know which is the right way to be Jewish?"

"I think you need to take things one step at a time," Rabbi Freeman replies. "Follow Hillel's advice—learn."

He smiles and his teeth flash white against his thick, brown beard.

"I have a feeling that if you keep learning you'll figure out what's the right way for you to be Jewish, much more effectively than if I sit here and tell you a whole list of things you should and shouldn't do."

He glances toward the buffet, where little Rivka is reaching for the cookie platter with two chocolaty hands.

"Why don't you stop by one day this week after school, and we can talk about this some more when—"

He jumps up and grabs the cookie plate, which is teetering on the edge of the table.

"Sorry. I had to rescue dessert," he says, sitting down again.

"No problem," I tell him. "You can jump up to rescue the brownies anytime. Chocolate is sacred to me."

I suddenly realize what I've said and wait for the rabbi to kick me out for sacrilege. But he just laughs.

"Judging by the state of my daughter's face and hands, I

think she feels the same way," he says. "Listen, come by this week—can you make Wednesday after school?"

I nod.

"Good. We'll talk about this some more and see if we can shed some light on the subject."

By the time I've finished eating, Mrs. Freeman has introduced me to most of the people there, and I've managed not to spill anything except for a few brownie crumbs. It must be a sign. Maybe this is where I belong.

Everyone is friendly and welcoming, and the brownies are to die for. I'm definitely going to come on Wednesday. Maybe even next Saturday, too.

Chapter Thirteen

I'm still feeling good, sort of uplifted, from my Sabbath experience when Jake shouts for me to get my butt downstairs for dinner the following evening. Sometimes I wonder where my parents went wrong with him; the kid has no manners. I quickly hide *Judaism for Dummies* under the covers and head down to the kitchen.

Mom's made lasagna, which is one of my favorites. But now I feel funny eating it. Bubbe wouldn't have lasagna unless it was vegetarian, because she didn't mix milk with meat. After going to services on Saturday and reading the library books, I've started to think about the whole kosher thing again. I'm having an internal debate about how I can bring it up to my parents without getting ridiculed, when Helena decides to grace us with her presence.

"Ugh! Meat Lasagna! Mom, you know I'm vegetarian," she says. "What did you make for me?"

"There's plenty of salad and vegetables, and if that's not enough you can make yourself a cheese sandwich," Mom says calmly. "I'm not a short-order chef, and this isn't a restaurant."

How does Helena get away with being vegetarian when I get laughed at for wanting to keep kosher? That's what I'd like to know.

Suddenly I get an idea. It's like in the cartoons when a lightbulb goes on above Bugs Bunny's head. I'll become a vegetarian like Helena! Then I won't have to worry about eating milk and meat together because I won't be eating meat at all.

Hamburgers are going to be hard; cheeseburgers even harder. Lasagna's going to be the hardest of all. I wonder if God will consider it a sin if I ask for seconds tonight, especially since I'm supposed to have given up meat for Lent. But I guess now that I've decided to be Jewish again, it doesn't really matter if I don't keep Lent. So this, I decide, will be my Last Supper with meat.

I'm so busy congratulating myself about my Divinely Inspired Solution that I'm totally unprepared when Helena drops the bomb.

"So what was Jussy doing coming out of that Center for Jewish Whatchamacallit place yesterday?" she says as she picks cherry tomatoes out of the salad. "Wasn't she supposed to be shopping with Mac?"

Mom puts down her fork and stares at me. Even Dad tears himself away from his food long enough to give me an inquiring look.

"Is this true, Justine? Was it you that Helena saw coming out of that place?" Mom asks quietly.

You'd have thought Helena said I came out of a bar singing, "Roll out the Barrel" and then danced the can-can naked in the center of town instead of exiting a house of worship—and one from our own religion, I might add. Imagine if Helena had seen me coming out of St. Clare's. Thank heaven for small mercies.

"It's not 'that place,'" I reply defiantly. "It's a synagogue. The people there are really nice. The food's good, too. They had *cholent* and lox and these amazing brownies and—"

"That's not the point," Mom interrupts irritably. "You told me that you were going shopping with Mac."

Sometimes my mother's logic is beyond me.

"Let me get this straight," I say. "You'd rather that I was shopping with Mac than going to synagogue?"

"That's not why I'm upset, Justine," Mom says through gritted teeth. "I'm hurt that you weren't honest about where you were going."

"Why on earth would you feel like you had to lie to your mother about such a thing?" asks Dad.

"Because . . ." I feel tears starting to well up and it makes me mad. "Because you guys never take me seriously, and I didn't want to be laughed at! That's why!"

I push away from the table and storm out of the kitchen

before Helena has a chance to make any snide comments. I hear Mom calling my name, but I ignore her and continue on upstairs.

I fling myself onto the bed, and brood about my family's insensitivity, clutching Bubbe's necklace in my hand. I miss her so much it hurts.

The bedroom door opens, and I brace myself for a lecture from Mom. But to my surprise it's my father. Dad usually avoids us when we're upset. I don't think he's comfortable dealing with all the emotional stuff, so he tends to leave it up to Mom.

"What's this all about, sweetheart?" he asks gently, sitting down on the bed and opening his arms.

I fling myself into his embrace. "I miss her, Daddy," I sob. "I miss her so much."

"I know, *bubbele,*" Dad says, stroking my hair. "So do I."

"She was there, Dad," I mumble into his shirt. "In the place I went yesterday. I felt her."

Why did I say that? Now Dad's going to think I'm a lunatic as well as a liar.

"Bubbe always had a special place in her heart for you, Jussy," Dad says. "I'm not surprised that you're the one she decided to visit first."

I look up at him, amazed. Parents can really surprise you sometimes. Just when you're expecting them to laugh at you or dial the number for the Funny Farm, they do the thing you expect the least—understand you.

Dad wipes away a tear on my cheek with his thumb.

"I'm surprised she hasn't come to give *me* an earful," he says with a wry smile. "I haven't been saying Kaddish."

"What do you mean?" I ask. "I thought you did it while we were sitting *shivah*."

"I did," he says. "But you're supposed to recite it three times a day for eleven months when a parent dies. It's meant to help their soul climb to the next level. Closer to God."

"I don't think Bubbe needs any help getting to heaven," I tell Dad. "She was good enough to get there on her own."

Dad smiles and ruffles my hair.

"You're right, sweetheart. Bubbe was a strong, determined lady. I bet she's up there right now, telling God how to run things better."

He sighs. "But I should still be saying Kaddish. It's part of fulfilling the commandment to 'honor thy father and mother.'"

Dad looks sad, so I give him a big hug. I think about how I would feel if both my parents were dead, like his are. Even though Dad's all grown up with his own kids, it still must be pretty awful for him to be an orphan. I hug him even harder. I don't want Dad to die. Ever.

"So I was thinking, Jussy, how about if I come with you to services next Sabbath? That way I can say Kaddish for Bubbe.

And who knows?" he says with a wry smile. "Maybe she'll come visit me, too."

"Yeah, she'll probably tell you to tuck in your shirt and stand up straighter," I say.

Dad laughs and gives me a squeeze.

I figure while Dad's being so unexplainably understanding and we're on the subject of religion, I might as well go for broke.

"Dad," I say hesitantly. "What would you say about me keeping kosher . . . like Bubbe did?"

Dad doesn't say anything, and I brace myself for ridicule, my family's standard response when I try to talk about things that are important to me.

But Dad surprises me again.

"Would keeping kosher mean something to you?" he asks. "More than just following a set of rules?"

"Yeah, it would," I tell him. "Especially now. It's kind of like you saying Kaddish. It would be my way of honoring Bubbe's memory. I think it would make her happy."

"There's no doubt about that," Dad says. "She was, shall we say, uh . . . *disappointed* when your mom and I didn't keep a kosher home."

"So why didn't you?" I asked.

"Well, your mother didn't grow up that way, and she's the one who runs the kitchen. I think she found the idea overwhelming. I didn't think it was that important, so we decided to forget about doing it," Dad replies. "In retrospect, it was probably a mistake."

"Why's that?" I ask.

"Because if you grow up keeping kosher, it's like second nature. You don't have to think about it. And you, Jake, and Helena don't have that now."

We both pause to think about it. I wonder if some of the tension I always sensed between Mom and Bubbe was because Bubbe was upset about the kosher thing. Maybe to Bubbe it seemed like Mom and Dad weren't respecting the stuff her family died for. But it's not like I can ask her now.

"Did Bubbe ever tell you about the time I came home from college wanting to be Buddhist?" Dad says.

"Yeah, she told me about the long hair and bell-bottoms, too!" I giggle.

Dad laughs. "Well, I was a lot thinner then. And I had a lot more hair. Imagine, Jussy, my hair was longer than yours!"

I try to imagine my balding father with hair as long as mine and giggle even more.

But Dad becomes serious. "Your Zayde told me, or rather shouted at me, that the laws of our faith are links in a chain, connecting us to our ancestors who received the Torah on Mount Sinai. He asked me if I had the chutzpah to break the chain, knowing that his family had all perished."

He sighs heavily. "I was headstrong and stubborn, convinced I knew everything. And I was sick of having 'what happened during the war' rammed down my throat all the time. I guess that gave me enough chutzpah."

"So . . . what do you think about me wanting to keep kosher?" I ask. "Do you think it's stupid?"

Dad puts his hands on my shoulders and kisses my forehead.

"Sweetheart, I couldn't be more proud," he says, giving me a hug. "I'll even smooth the way with your mother. Now come down and have some dinner."

I feel a warm glow from his words, and it feels like there are three people hugging me, Dad and two other shadowy presences, Bubbe and Zayde. We head downstairs for the Last Supper. I eat three helpings of lasagna.

Chapter Fourteen

True to his word, Dad has a long talk with Mom about me keeping kosher. We even sit in the living room to discuss it the following night. I think it's the first time I've been alone in the living room with my parents where they're not mad at me about something. It's like they're actually taking me seriously for a change and discussing the idea with me like I'm a grown-up. Best of all, when Helena and Jake try to butt their noses in, Mom tells them to leave, because it's a private discussion between her and Dad and me. I know it's childish and I'm supposed to be mature because they're treating me like a grown-up for a change, but I can't resist sticking my tongue out at Jake when Mom's back is turned. I'll have to put it on my Yom Kippur Repentance List, which is already a page and a half long.

We agree that I'll start off being vegetarian during the week and that Mom will order the Shabbat Chicken Meal to be delivered from the kosher deli so I can have meat once a week.

"In a way it's good for me, too," Mom says. "It'll be a proper day of rest for me because I don't have to cook."

Now that all my issues of faith are out of the closet, I don't have to lie to Mom about going to see Rabbi Freeman on Wednesday afternoon. She drops me off at the Jewish Understanding Center and takes Jake for hot chocolate and homework at Starbucks while I talk to the rabbi.

He ushers me into his office and tells me to take a seat in a comfortable chair facing his desk.

"You look a bit nervous," he says as he sits down. "There's no need to be."

"Yeah, I suppose," I say. "I mean you already know the worst of my sins anyway, right?"

He leans back in his chair and starts to stroke his beard.

"You know something, Justine?" he says. "You need to change your focus a bit. You're concentrating on the concept of sin too much."

"I am?" I ask, amazed. "But I thought we were supposed to think about that stuff."

Rabbi Freeman smiles.

"Look, I'm not saying you shouldn't think about it at all, or that you should rush out and do things the Torah says are wrong," he says. "But I also don't think it helps to think of God as some kind of heavenly Terminator who's waiting for you to sin so he can mete out some dire punishment."

He leans forward in his chair. "Do your parents ever punish you?"

The question takes me by surprise.

"Well, yeah," I say. "I mean, they're parents. It's their job."

The rabbi laughs.

"Well, yes, it is their job," he says. "The Talmud says 'You should discipline a child with the left hand and draw him closer with the right.' Your parents discipline you because they love you and want to teach you right from wrong. They never stop loving you. I hope you can start to think of God that way."

"I never thought of God like that, you know, like a parent," I tell the rabbi. "I hope He's not going to start telling me to clean up my room and that I shouldn't eat chocolate because it'll make me fat."

Rabbi Freeman chuckles and leans back in his chair again. "That's one of the wonderful things about Judaism, Justine," he says. "You don't need to feel torn between your spirituality on the one hand and your material desires, like say for"—he smiles—"chocolate. The sages say nothing is higher than delight."

"They do?" I ask, incredulous. "You mean I don't have to

feel guilty about wanting to eat chocolate? It's not like . . . gluttony or anything?"

Rabbi Freeman laughs. "It only depends on how you eat it," he says.

I guess I look as clueless as I feel.

"Okay, let's look at your confusion about, how'd you put it? 'The Right Way to Be Jewish.'"

"That's exactly it!" I exclaim, hoping that he's finally going to solve the mystery of how I'm supposed to be Jewish but not too Jewish and yet still be true to the things that Bubbe's family, all those great aunts, uncles, and cousins that I never knew, died for.

"It's clear to me that you have a strong sense of spirituality," the rabbi says, and I feel a warm glow. First Father Joe tells me I'm 'a Girl with Faith,' and now the rabbi's telling me I'm a spiritual girl. I feel like Madonna—oh wait, she's the *material girl*.

"I wonder if part of your confusion about how to be Jewish comes because you've seen your Bubbe perform the 'how' of observance, but you've never been taught the 'whys' of it," suggests the rabbi.

"What, you mean like why we light the menorah on Hanukkah and stuff like that? I learned all that at Hebrew school," I tell him.

"That's a start," Rabbi Freeman says, "but I'm talking about an even deeper, more fundamental level."

"Like what?" I ask.

"Like the *mitzvahs,* the observances that we do, are a means to connect heaven and earth. They allow us to heal the rift between our physical and our spiritual selves, between the material and spiritual parts of our being."

I'm trying to digest this, with very little success, when he finally puts it into language that I can understand.

"Let's take chocolate," he says, and opening his desk drawer, he takes out a box of chocolates with Hebrew writing on the front. He offers one to me, and takes one for himself.

"There's nothing wrong with wanting to eat chocolate," he says, smiling.

"Phew! That's a relief," I say.

I'm about to take a bite when he says, "Do you mind waiting a moment, Justine, before you eat it? It's part of the explanation."

"Sorry," I say, and I can feel myself blushing.

"Not to worry," he says gently. Holding up his piece of chocolate, the rabbi asks me to repeat a Hebrew blessing after him. Then he pops the chocolate in his mouth and nods for me to do the same.

We both sit there chewing, enjoying the sweetness on our tongues.

"You see, Justine," says the rabbi when he finishes chewing, "by saying that little blessing, we transformed the simple act of eating a chocolate, the desire for which comes from our physical selves, into a means of connecting with the divine spark within us."

"Wow," I say. "I've always thought of eating chocolate as a religious experience, but this gives it a whole new light."

"That's it!" Rabbi Freeman exclaims.

I've got the clueless face on again. I'm sure of it.

"*What's* it?"

"To give ordinary, material things a whole new 'light,' by using the *mitzvahs,* or observances, God gave us to bridge the two facets of our soul, the material and the spiritual," he explains. "What's more, if you use the energy you get from your delight in eating chocolate to do a *mitzvah,* or a good deed, it brings you closer to God."

I don't know if it's because of the chocolate, the blessing, or the rabbi's explanation, but suddenly I get a glimmer of understanding. Just a little one, I'll admit, but a glimmer all the same.

"So, Rabbi, if I say the blessing again, can I have another chocolate?" I ask.

He laughs and hands me the box. "You don't need to say another blessing, but here, help yourself to a chocolate. In fact, you've done so well today, take two."

Chapter Fifteen

Dad comes with me to services at the Center for Jewish Understanding on Saturday morning. He says Kaddish for Bubbe and makes arrangements for Rabbi Freeman to say it during morning services, even if Dad can't be there. Afterward, Dad says he'll come to services with me every Saturday if I want to go. I'm not sure if it's because of wanting to say Kaddish, or because he liked the *cholent* and brownies. I'm just happy to be there with my dad.

I'm really excited when the Weinsteins' car pulls into the driveway the following morning. It seems like years since I've seen Shira, and I've got so much to tell her.

Shira's getting out of the car when I run out of the back door, and I fling myself into her arms.

"It's so good to see you!" I exclaim.

"Ditto," she says.

Then, over her shoulder, I see someone climbing out of the car. It's the cutest guy I've ever seen, with curly dark hair and eyes as blue as the water you see on posters for the Caribbean.

"You remember my cousin Robert, don't you, Jussy?" Shira says casually, unaware that I've been hit by a serious case of cousin-lust. I remember Rob all right, but as a skinny guy with braces and glasses, not . . . this.

"And here's Amie," Shira adds as Rob's younger sister comes around from the other side of the car with Sammy.

"Nice to see you again, Justine," Rob says, and he smiles, revealing straight, braceless teeth. Oh boy. This is definitely not the Robert that I remember. No sirree.

"Uh . . . hi, Rob . . . uh . . . hi, Amie," I manage to stutter. My face feels 212 degrees hot, and I know I must look and sound like a total dork. Why is it that when I want to be the least dorky I seem to reach ever higher levels of dorkitude?

We go inside for brunch. When Helena joins us, my heart sinks, because as usual she looks picture-perfect and I know that one look at her and Rob is going to forget I exist; if he ever took note of the fact in the first place, that is. But when we've all loaded up our plates and go into the family room to eat, Rob comes and sits next to me on the sofa. It almost makes me lose my appetite because I'm so afraid of accidentally choking and spraying him with lox.

I'm really glad Shira and Amie are there, because their

bubbly chatter covers up the fact that I am too nervous to say a word in case I sound stupid in front of Rob. Helena comes in with her plate of salad and sits down in the chair next to him. *She* doesn't have any problems striking up a conversation. I figure that now Helena's talking to him I don't have a chance, because he's going to fall in love with her like all the boys do, even if to him she's an older woman. For some reason, this makes me feel even more miserable than when Mac told me Tommy was dating Athena Johnson, and that was miserable enough for me, thank you.

I feel myself sinking into a haze of gloom. I'm torn between not wanting to eat at all and wanting to skip the bagels and go straight for the brownies.

"Jussy . . . Jussy . . . Earth to Justine Silver," Shira calls playfully in my ear, putting a temporary halt on my misery spiral. "Where were you just now? Not on this planet, that's for sure."

I give her a weak smile, but she's too good a friend to be fooled by it.

"Hey, what's up?" she asks quietly. Then she notices the necklace. "Wow! Jussy! Where did you get that gorgeous necklace? I've never seen you wear it, I'm sure of it. I'd remember seeing something that beautiful."

"I noticed it, too," Amie says. "It's really pretty."

Robert turns from his conversation with Helena. "Let's see," he says, and he reaches toward my neck and gently lifts the star into his hand. I feel his warm fingers briefly touch my neck, and almost drop my plate.

"That's beautiful," he says, and he looks from the necklace to my face. I can feel the blush starting and am mesmerized by his eyes, like Mowgli and Kaa the snake in the *Jungle Book* movie. "I think it's great you're proud to be Jewish. Most of the girls I know seem to spend all their time pretending they're something they're not."

Ouch. Just when I was starting to feel better, I'm hit by a ten-ton weight of guilt, because I know that I've been one of those girls.

Mr. Blab-It-All, a.k.a. Jake, pipes up, "Yeah, like Jussy wanting to be—"

"Jake!" Helena cuts him off abruptly, before he's able to spill the secret of my closet Catholicism. "Why don't you go get a carton of orange juice?"

I feel an unusual rush of gratitude toward my sister for saving me from instant mortification.

"Get it yourself," Jake retorts rudely, "Jussy and I set the table."

"I'll get it," Amie says sweetly, starting to get up from the floor.

Jake turns bright red and mutters, "Uh, that's okay, Amie. I'll get it," but he can't help adding in an undertone as he passes by Helena, "for *Amie.* Not for *you.*"

"So where'd you get the necklace, Jussy?" Sammy asks.

"It was from Bubbe. She . . ."

That familiar prickly feeling is starting up in my eyes. I really, really don't want to cry in front of Rob, so I put my plate on the coffee table so I can leave the room, but I accidentally put it on the TV remote control and the plate slides off onto Rob's leg, decorating his jeans with cream cheese and lox.

"Oh God! I'm sorry. I'm *so* sorry!" I say, throwing a napkin on his cream-cheesy leg. I know I should stay to help him clean himself off, but I'm so embarrassed and miserable I just want to leave. I push my way past Shira's legs and end up knocking over her orange juice.

It's the last straw. I burst into full-fledged crying.

"I can't believe it!" I wail. Sobbing, I run out of the room. As I leave I hear Jake saying, "That's my sister Jussy for you . . . leaving chaos in her wake," and Helena telling him to shut up and make himself useful by going to get something to clean up with.

I escape to my room and throw myself on the bed, curled up in a little ball around Father Ted. I wonder if I'm ever going to be normal, or if I'm always going to be the fat, ugly girl who spills things.

There's a knock on the door.

"Don't come in!" I shout.

But like a good friend, Shira ignores me and comes in anyway. She sits down on the bed and rubs my back. She doesn't say anything right away, just lets me cry it all out. Then, just when I've got to the hiccuping stage, she says, "You know, Jussy, that's a lot of crying for a spilled orange juice."

I give one of those crying snorts, the kind that makes all the snot come out of your nose, and I'm glad that it's only Shira there to see it.

"Can you be a useful friend and pass me a tissue?" I sniff. "Besides, it wasn't just spilled orange juice—I had to cry about the bagel and cream cheese, too."

Shira hands me a tissue and lies down on the pillow next to me.

"Look at the bright side," she says philosophically. "You could have spilled a brownie and wasted perfectly good chocolate."

"Shira." I sniff gratefully. "What would I do without you to remind me what's really important in life?"

There's another knock on the door. Can't people let a girl be miserable in peace?

"Uh . . . Justine? It's Rob. I just wanted to make sure you're all right . . . Is it okay to come in?"

Ohmigod! The gorgeous Robert is outside my bedroom door, covered in cream cheese, and I'm in here looking like Rudolph the Red-Nosed Reindeer. Proof, if any were needed, that there is no justice in this world, especially when your name is Justine Frieda Silver.

I hastily sit up and dry my eyes, then tell him to come in. The first thing I notice is the large, white smear on the leg of his jeans. He sees where I'm looking and smiles.

"I would have asked for seconds if I'd really wanted them," he says. "And, I prefer onion bagels to sesame seed. Just so you know for next time."

Next time? He said, "Next time." Does that mean he doesn't wish I'll be exiled to somewhere remote and freezing where there's no chocolate?

He sits down on the other side of me. "Move over, Shira, you're taking up the whole bed."

"It's just because you're such a hulking lump, Rob, you need so much space," Shira retorts. "By the way, did anyone ever tell you that your aftershave smells remarkably like lox?"

I start giggling uncontrollably. Sometimes that happens after I've been crying, almost like things need to balance themselves out.

"What's so funny?" Helena asks as she walks into my room. "Here I come to comfort my little sister, and I find you up here having a party without me. A girl could take this personally."

"Don't," Shira says. "You know what they say: *If you can't beat 'em, join 'em.*"

Helena plonks herself on the bed. It's starting to get kind

of crowded, but it's been a long time since Helena's come into my room for anything except to yell at me for borrowing her clothes, so I'm enjoying it. She even stuck up for me today—twice. Maybe she's not such a bad big sister after all.

"So, Jussy, let's hear about this necklace," says Shira, fingering it.

Helena shoots me a worried look, like she's afraid that I'm going to start crying again. But I know Shira well enough to know she's not going to give up until she's heard all the gory details. "Inquiring Minds Want to Know" and all that.

"Bubbe left it to me," I tell Shira and Rob. "In her will. She wrote me a letter."

I get up and find the lacquered box that my dad brought back from a business trip to Hong Kong. It's where I keep all my most treasured possessions. Rob leans over Shira's shoulder as she reads Bubbe's letter out loud. I pick up Father Ted and pace around the room clutching him tightly.

"What's all this about wanting to be Catholic?" Shira asks in astonishment. "Are you serious? I thought you liked being Jewish?"

I'd forgotten about that part. Urgent Message to Brain: *Start thinking fast because now I have to explain.*

"Well . . . I . . ." I try to think of some explanation other than the truth, but can't. So I tell them all about Father Ted, the rosary beads, and my closet confessional. By the time I get to the part about the mice and the Anytime Anywhere Pest Service blowing my cover, Shira and Rob are in fits of laughter.

"I'd have loved to have seen your mom's face when she saw the mouse in her closet," Shira gasps between giggles. "I mean, she's more uptight about cleanliness than anyone I know. She makes my mom look like a grade-A slob!"

"Justine, you're priceless," Rob says, in what I hope is an admiring way. "A real original thinker. It's so cool that you took the time to learn about another religion. Knowledge makes people more tolerant. Too bad more people don't do what you did, and learn about different beliefs."

I feel myself blushing. Could it be that he doesn't hate me for pretending to be something I'm not, like those other girls he knows?

"Your parents must have freaked!" Shira says wonderingly.

"They did," Helena tells her grimly. "But somehow you didn't seem to get punished too much," she says, looking at me curiously. "How did you get away with it?"

"It was Bubbe. She defended me to Mom and Dad," I tell her. "I'm not sure if I'll ever understand why, especially when it must have hurt her so much."

Rob picks up Bubbe's letter and reads aloud: "'So, Jussy darling, I hope someday you will wear this necklace and that it will give you as much pleasure as knowing you has given me. When you put it on, you'll know that Zayde and I are up in heaven, smiling. Remember, even if we aren't physically present, we'll always be there watching over you and surrounding you with our love. No one could have asked for a more wonderful granddaughter.'"

By the time he finishes, we're all crying. At least all of us girls, but even Rob's eyes are glistening.

"It sounds to me like your grandmother thought you were one very special girl," he says. "She's right, you know," he adds softly.

Through my tears I hear his words and feel warm deep inside.

"She's so special," sings Shira in her extremely off-key voice, and we all start cracking up.

Later that afternoon, when it's time for the Weinsteins to leave, Rob takes me aside.

"Listen, Justine, I hope you're feeling better. Don't worry about my pants. My mom owns pretty much every stain remover known to man."

"Hey, she should meet my mom. They could have coffee and compare cleaning products."

Rob smiles with those wonderful white braceless teeth. "You've got such a great sense of humor."

Then he hesitates and I'm amazed to see that he's blushing.

"So . . . um . . . Jussy. Would you mind if I called you sometime?" he asks tentatively.

Would I mind? What, is he nuts?

"Uh . . . yeah. I'd like that," I tell him, and I can feel myself blushing, too.

"Great!" Rob says, sounding both happy and relieved. He gives me a quick peck on the cheek, and then runs out to the car where the Weinsteins are waiting.

I stand there for a minute, holding my hand to the spot where his lips touched my cheek, and wonder if I can wash my face around it. With my luck I'd probably just end up with a huge zit. Sighing, I head outside to join the others.

We all stand on the porch to wave good-bye. Helena puts her arm around me.

"He's pretty cute, that Rob," she whispers in my ear so Jake doesn't hear. "I think he likes you, too."

I think of him asking if he can call me, and touch the magic spot on my right cheek. "You're right," I say to her, smiling. "I think he does."

The next day at school, I hand Mac her silver cross necklace and tell her that I found it under my bedside table. I feel guilty about lying, but I've put it on the ever-growing Yom Kippur Repentance List, now several pages long.

Mac's happy I found her necklace.

"My parents gave it to me at my first Communion," she says. "I was really sad when I'd thought I'd lost it."

I tell Mac about Bubbe's necklace and the letter.

"You were really lucky to have a grandmother like Bubbe," Mac says.

"I know," I tell her.

"But you know something, Jussy?" Mac continues. "She was really lucky to have such a special granddaughter. And she knew it, too."

"Thanks, Mac," I say gratefully.

"Now enough of that or your head won't fit back into the classroom," Mac teases. "Anyway, I want to hear more about this Rob of yours."

I start to tell her about Rob and how he asked if I would mind if he called me. As I do, I feel a strange, warm glow, and I can't help thinking that it's Bubbe and Zayde up in heaven together, smiling.

Glossary of Yiddish and Hebrew Terms

bubbe (BUB-ee): grandmother

bubbele (BUB-eh-leh): literally, "little grandmother" (a term of endearment)

challah (HA-lah): braided loaf of bread eaten on the Sabbath

Chumash (HUM-ash): Five Books of Moses (Old Testament)

chutzpah (HUTZ-pah): nerve, gall

Ess! (es): Eat!

goniff (GONE-if): thief

Kaddish (CA-dish): a prayer for the Jewish soul, recited by mourners

kinderlach (KIN-dair-lach): children

klutz (rhymes with "butts"): clumsy person

maidel (MAY-del): girl

mammele (MA-meh-leh): literally, "little mother" (a term of endearment)

mishegas (mish-eh-GOSS): craziness

Shabbat shalom (Hebrew)(sha-BAT sha-LOM): Sabbath peace

shayne (SHAY-neh): pretty

shayne punim (SHAY-neh POON-im): pretty face

Shema (sh-MAH): The most important prayer in the Jewish liturgy: "Hear, O Israel, the Lord is our God, the Lord is One."

shul (shool): synagogue

tchotchkes (CHOCH-kehs): knickknacks

Torah (TOR-ah): scrolls containing the Five Books of Moses

zayde (ZAY-deh): grandfather